I0461636

RIVERS OF FORTITUDE

FORT WAYNE AMATEUR WRITER'S PROJECT 2007

Issue 1
Volume 1

1ˢᵗ edition

Copyright © 2007 Fort Wayne Amateur Writers Project
Committee

All rights reserved.
Each Author retains the copyright to their respective works contained
herein. No part of this book may be reproduced or transmitted in any
form other or by any means whatsoever, except in the case of brief
excerpts quoted in reviews, without permission in writing from the
Publisher or the individual author of said work.

ISBN - 978-0-6151-7817-2

Cover design by Matt Presswood

All proceeds go towards producing next year's collection.
writefw@gmail.com
www.fwawp.com

CONTENTS

Brian Landrum

This collection of literature is proof that good things can happen on a collaborative level. It took awhile, but here it is. Things were a bit deranged at the beginning. Once the submissions started in however, it was obvious that this was something that had to succeed. There were good writers waiting to be read. Things almost fell apart a few times. Either the finances were lacking or personal situations threw my attentions elsewhere. Once Amber and Matt got involved, things got on the right track and the project was reconceived. Without them, you wouldn't be holding this book right now. Most importantly, none of this would have been possible without the efforts of Fort Wayne's creative talent. Thank you for supporting them and the overall enrichment of this community. See you next issue.

Jess

    Credit should certainly be given where it is due, and Jess has been the brains behind this wonderful Project. It has been a pleasure to work on compiling and editing what will be the first of many editions of "The Fort Wayne Amateur Writer's Project." My hope for this Project is to eventually create a network of local writers and artists; to bring people together in an atmosphere of creative and supportive energy. Please log onto the website to get involved or give feedback. You should feel proud, dear reader, to be a part of the beginning of this adventure.

Amber

Christmas for Harry
Shaun Bryan

She moves in such symmetrical perfection. When she spins, her arms leave her body in swift moments of fluidity, underneath the dim light of the dance studio. And her students, all young and pretending to be her, watch as her body collapses and rebirths itself in soft moves like a smooth storm.

As I'm passing by her tonight I stop in front of the window where she's dancing and look up into the bright lights of the streetlamps and watch the snow slowly materialize from the dark sky and twirl through the air in gentle circular motions. They try and escape me and rest against the icy concrete sidewalks but they become entangled in my dirty beard like tiny nesting birds.

I pretend that she and I are in a snow globe, secluded from the rest of the world and that the snow will perpetually fall down to me and I just stand outside watching her dance, separated by bricks and glass windows for eternity.

When the class is over the children scatter to their parents and they walk home. She turns off the lights and moves through the dark studio and reappears in the cold night to lock the doors from the outside. I pretend to be looking through trash so she won't notice me and she doesn't. She also doesn't notice that I see her stick her tongue out to catch a snowflake on it as she makes her way across the street dodging taxi cabs and frozen puddles of water.

I follow her home to make sure she stays safe. It isn't long before she kisses her husband and draws the shades, leaving me only the shadows to watch fall asleep, the television lighting up the room like an indecisive candle and I walk through the abandoned subway system where there is a cold wet corner that I call home.

All of the faces I pass are familiar. Faces that look as if life has melted hot grief across their skin, leaving deep scarring lines of dejection. As if an unbearable weight has been tattooed into the very fiber of their muscles. Flames choke out the darkness in deep crevices and passages as they are held up to glass pipes and the softly illuminated faces laugh high-pitched melancholy cackles through cocaine eyes.

My corner is comfortable, with layer upon layer of blankets, one on top of the other like a stack of warm coziness. I keep a bucket next to me that catches the water which drips from the leaky pipe that runs above us all, through the tunnel. When I brush my teeth I can taste the coppery rust of the pipes mingling with the mint toothpaste. I also keep a box nearby where everything that I treasure is kept safely locked away, and only I have the key.

All of my other belongings are in a bag that I carry around with me. It's sturdy and has a sun stitched into the tough fabric. I pull out my candle and light it, watch the wax drip down from the hot flame that's slowly digesting the wick and drift into the hypnotic dance of the flame because it helps me get what's in my head to my notebook.

Slowly lights begin to go out in the tunnel. Everyone is getting ready to wake up tomorrow and get a head start before all of the mornings garbage has been gathered and eaten. I don't sleep much. Not because it's too cold or I'm worried about someone stealing my things, but because I have insomnia. I usually just take cat naps during the day on benches for short bursts of time. My favorite time is coming home to the tunnel and sitting by the candlelight and writing. I don't have much use for the day. She doesn't begin her dance lessons until after the sunlight has been long extinguished and the moon has taken over watch on the city.

It's strange, the hypnotic power of something so simple as firelight. I stare and stare until suddenly the world around me begins to dim and fuzz over like the edges of overexposed film. The sounds I hear become fainter and drift off until all you hear is the silence that could only come from somewhere inside your head. Then your thoughts twist and twirl around for a moment or so until all thinking is completely eliminated and you're left to be free from reality and simply exist.

I'm doing this, really intent on the flame because everything else has disappeared and for a second it's like I'm sucked inside the flame and we are the same but I still see it, dancing around and around and around, waltzing across the pupils of my eyes. Then Damien sits down next to me and I drift back to myself and take the cup of coffee that he's offering me.

Damien is the oldest person I know. He's on a methadone program at the clinic because he's been addicted to heroin since he was twenty-three. Damien has told me that the reason he's lived so long is that heroin kills off your blood cells and forces your body to replenish them so he's constantly being reborn. He tells me he could live forever if he wanted to but when his body gets too old to carry him through the day he'll probably just decide to die.

We both drink the coffee in silence, staring at the flame as he runs his fingers over in and out of the dimples of the coarse cover of the Bible which he always carries with him. He's also the most religious man I know. His father was a preacher and he claims that he's never missed a Sunday mass in his life. Even when his father found out that he was using drugs and disowned him, claiming that the devil and demons stole his son from him, he still found a different church to go to and has every Sunday since.

For some reason I start thinking about this and ask him, "Do you ever think that you'll change your mind about God and stop going to church, Damien?"

He speaks slow and his voice is very deep and sounds strangled as if his vocal chords are threatening to give out on him at any second. "Church... isn't about God to me anymore Harry." His lips quiver in between his sentences as he tells me this. "I walk home from the clinic sometimes and the world is filled with people and all they have are these...routines. For some...it's watching their favorite television programs... or... jogging in the park. And these people... they look forward to these things. It's what makes them wake up and get out of their beds in the...morning. Church is my routine. It's something to look forward to. The heroin is what made me feel the closest to God. Losing one made me lose the other."

"But, you're on the methadone now," I say.

Damien runs his worn hands over the wrinkles on his weathered face and tries to stand up but I have to help him. Before he leaves he puts his arm on my shoulder and says, "Harry... the difference between heroin and methadone is the same as the difference between you watching that woman dance... and holding her in your arms."

I watch as his frail skinny frame disappears and put my notebook back into my bag and blow out the candle. Lying down I stare into the blackness around me for hours before I finally fall asleep.

***

Sally and I are drunk on cheap port wine underneath railroad tracks that run through the city. She just found out that she was accepted into a program that she's been trying to get into where the government is going to give her free housing for some months until either she or they find her a job. I don't how she got the wine. Maybe she stole it or maybe she hustled enough money today to buy it. She got to see the apartment that she's going to be living in today and as she's telling me all about it as she cradles the heavy glass jug of wine in her arms and spins around in circles at the moments when she is overcome with elation. She has this huge, contagious, toothless smile that makes her face rumple itself into ecstasy.

"Izz gotta kichen Harry and ooooh, you shud see duh batroom. Dat tub be big enuff fur da bofe 'a us. I be livin' da high life, ha ha. Ain't got no betroom doh. Dey callit 'a stu-dio, but dey says dey gonna furnish it wit everytang I gonna need."

The glass of the bottle gleams in the moonlight and reflects in her eyes and she fades in and out of sight, her black skin melding with the dark night. The liquor sits in my belly and I feel it coarse through my body, warming me from the inside out. The sound of an oncoming train whistle busts through air and the roar of its' steel wheels against the rails above us wash over our bodies like fists of sound. Sally closes her eyes and rocks back and forth to the rhythm of the passing train and I see her singing to herself.

The sound slowly subsides away from us and into the city and it suddenly seems so silent in its absence. Sally passes me the bottle of wine and says, in a voice you only use when you are remembering something, "my Grammy used ta sang dat song to me."

"What song's that Sally?"

"She calltit da train song." And then she sings a verse of it for me:
"Dat lonesome train,
Dat you been chasin' in da rain,
Oooooh, dat lonesome train,
You can dream bout catchin' dat lonesome train,
But you cain't neva keep yuh footin' when it rain."

"Maybe when dey gimme my place I can git my boy back, and den I can sing *him* dat song.

"Anything is possible," I tell her, and I watch as she sits on the cold ground, leans against the concrete of the bridge and slowly falls asleep singing to herself in a silent voice.

***

I probably hear them before anyone else around me does because I'm still awake when they come. I see the flashlights hit the walls and spread out like a ripple in water. The police have come again. They shout in angry voices and hold their nightsticks in their free hands looking for us. They hunt us and we're helpless to stop them. They scream that this is public property and that we can't stay here. If we fail to leave we'll be arrested. Gather our belongings and evacuate the area now.

I put my box in my bag with my notebooks and make sure that I have the key. One of them kicks one of us because he's so drunk he can't wake up. Some of us help him get himself up and hold him up to walk him out. Some of them are covering their mouths because of the way we smell. They shine their flashlights in our homes and rummage through the belongings that we have left, making sure not to touch anything with their hands.

4

Some of us that haven't been here long enough to know better won't come back. Those of us that have been here long enough know that they do this and that there's no way for them to keep us out. We'll come back and then leave again when they come back. This is just the way it works. We all go up the stairs single file like Jews in a concentration camp. We exit into the night and the wind whips against us like razor blades across our faces.

Everyone goes their separate ways, some of us in pairs or small groups. You always have a back-up. You have to. We all have our secret spots for times like this or when you just can't get home. We saunter off in what feels like helpless defeat.

She isn't at the dance studio. It's just a dark empty room without her to fill it with her light. Tomorrow she'll be dancing by herself. Practicing her moves and I'll watch.

I smell Chinese stir-fry in the air, the tender meat being seared in a hot wok and the vegetables fried until their skin is a dark brown. My stomach ties itself into a knot and I nearly double over in pain. It feels as though someone has plunged a drill into my guts and is slowly pulling the trigger over and over, twisting them into a coiled mass of hunger. I can barely walk because I'm so hungry.

In the back of the restaurant I lift the lid to the dumpster and can barely see inside but still rifle through the trash looking for something to eat. I see something round in the shadows and have to nearly get inside to get it so I rest my waist on the hard side of the dumpster and lean into it, the round object barely out of reach. I go further and further in until I'm practically walking on my hands, inching my way through the spoiled and rotten food remnants, noodles working their way through my fingers like worms. My finger tip touches its' smooth round surface. I pinch the side and pull it forward and it rolls towards me through the trash and into my hand. Once I've gotten a good hold on it, pull it and myself out of the trash and hold the ball of cabbage up to the alley lights. It's a little brown but still edible. I find a dark corner were no one will see me and eat it. It tastes delicious. Only the outer layer was bad, inside its all green and still crispy and crunchy in my mouth. The pain in my stomach leaves in gratitude. I even find almost a whole cigarette sitting next to me, but it's wet from the icy damp ground so I have to let it dry out before I light it. When I do, the smoke fills my lungs, the menthol coating my chest in like an icy feeling that reminds me of being young and stealing my mother's cigarettes when she wasn't around.

The streets are becoming empty and the shops are all closing but they leave the display window lights on, decorated in reds and greens with wreaths and blinking lights winding around the displays. From some far off speaker I hear a distorted version of "Jingle Bells" echoing into the air. I love this time of year.

I see the neon lights of the all-night diner radiating in a sea of the empty closed wasteland of shops and restaurants. Damien and some other familiar faces are inside so I go in and sit next to him. The cook standing behind the counter gives me a dirty look, but not long after I sit down a waitress puts an empty mug in front of me and fills it with steaming coffee. "I don't have any money," I tell her.

"I know," she says through a smile and walks away to fill someone else's cup.

"Do you have somewhere to stay tonight, Damien?"

"Yes… I've called someone and they've unlocked the church for me. They've told me I could stay until morning. Do you have someplace…to go?"

"I think so," I tell him, but I really don't. I know of plenty places I could sleep, but none of them are warm.

"Tomorrow is Christmas Eve Harry."

"I know."

"The soup kitchen is going to be feeding all of us. Would you like to…have dinner with me tomorrow?" Damien is smiling, laughing at himself. It's funny, but not in the way jokes used to be funny. The jokes that we tell now are just comments that make light of our situation. It helps us get through moments of despair.

"Yes," I say, "dinner sounds lovely tomorrow. I also know an excellent place on the nickel that serves and excellent prime rib."

"No," Damien says, "I think that soup will do just fine."

I know that tomorrow Damien will go to midnight mass like he does every year and that he'll ask me if I'd like to go with him and maybe I will this year. Just for him.

We all drink our coffees and I listen in on conversations going on around me. We all tell stories of Christmas's that we've had. Some are sad, but the ones from when we were young are told with fondness, in voices that ring out in a slightly higher register than the normal tones of dejection.

The diner is filled with only us for some time but when a family comes in from the cold streets to have dinner the cook behind the counter gives us the look that we've come to know so well. It's the look that means we have to leave. The look that says, "he's done what he can for us, but he has a business to run and we know as well as he does that we just aren't good for business."

We all leave single file again, but not like the persecuted Jews we once were, but kings, our bellies full of coffee and our spirits lifted just in time for Christmas Eve. Outside, Damien tells me, "come with me Harry, I have something for you." I follow him down the street. He walks slowly, but I don't mind. We don't say anything to each other, just walk in silence with our own thoughts.

We finally stop in front of a huge church, decorated with tall intimidating statues of Jesus and Mary. They stand over me high into the air for what seems like miles above my head. All of them look so sad. As if they're crying but no tears will ever run out of the hard stone structures. And that made me sad to think about. All of these people trapped forever in a pose of deep sadness never able to see all the beauty that passes by them in the world, right outside the church steps.

"I told you I have a place to sleep tonight."

"I know," he says. "That isn't why I brought you here."

I follow him up the marble steps of the church and the statues follow me in with their stone eyes. He opens the door and we step inside and he turns the locks on the doors behind us. The lights are off and I can't see anything until he flips a switch and suddenly the stained glass windows and pews that lead up to the alter are lit up in a vibrant white light.

"This way," Damien says, leading up stairs that were hidden behind a hallway behind us. "I must…confess." He takes each step slowly, making sure he doesn't fall and break his frail body. "I actually brought you here out of selfishness because it's something I want from you."

We reach the second story of the church and he opens a huge purple velvet curtain and we step on to a balcony that overlooks the entire place. In front of us is one of the most beautiful pipe organs I'd ever seen. It has etchings all over it of leaves and vines that entwine along its' mahogany body. Damien flips a switch on it and I hear the air rustle through it and it sounds as if it's coming to life. He sits down in a chair next to the organ and crosses his arms. "I'd like my Christmas present from you tonight Harry. Preferably some Bach if that's possible."

I slowly sit down to the organ, almost scared. I haven't played in years and Damien knows this, but he also knows about my past. I run my fingers across the black and white keys, admiring the sexy contrast of colors that it had been so long since I'd seen and felt. I place my feet on the pedals on the floor and pump it up and down, getting a feel for them, listening to them creak and moan from age. My heart beats in my chest faster and faster in anxiety until I play the first notes and it slowly settles down and I close my eyes when the sound fills the church, bouncing off the walls and filling the air with Bach's "Fugue in D minor." The notes curl and flow through me and out of my fingertips and any thoughts I harbored about not being able to play anymore are vanquished once I drift off to concert halls that I once filled.

When I finish the piece I look over to Damien who's fallen asleep on the chair, his chest rising and falling in slow-motion, in between deep shallow breaths. I take one last look at the organ and turn off the switch and the hum that once the room slowly fades out of existence, leaving nothing but silence and the sound of our breathing. I try to fall asleep in the comfort of the church but my insomnia is persistent. Sometime around dawn I go back home, back to my corner and my blankets. Back to my notebook and my candle. Back to my present, for her.

***

I meet Damien at the church just before midnight and we sit in the back and wait for the sermon. All of the families are dressed in their best clothes, with thick warm coats and hats that match their outfits and some have gloves that match their hats. They all smell delicious, like cinnamon and gingerbread. When the man in the robes comes out everyone stands up and waits as he slowly makes his way to the pulpit. He says in a kind voice, "peace be with you."

Everyone responds, "and also with you," and we sit. I haven't been to church in years. He speaks of things like giving and unselfishness and I listen, but my favorite parts are when the organ player plays songs in between the important parts of the evening. At one point we all form a line and make our way to the front of the church where we have to eat a wafer and drink wine from a cup. Damien says it's called communion and I just do whatever he does. The man in the robes holds out the cup for me to drink from and looks down on me with caring eyes while I just feel helpless and dirty, sitting on my knees, so far below him.

We sit down again, far in the back away from everyone else until it's over. The people are all leaving, children holding their mother's hands. I look over at Damien wondering if we should leave with them or wait until their all gone but he isn't conscious. He dozes in and out because of the methadone. I tug on his arm a little to try and get him up but he doesn't move. I call his name to him but he doesn't respond. I notice the absence of his deep shallow breaths which are always so distinct and disturbing and even though he has layers and layers of clothes on beneath his heavy coat, I know that he isn't breathing. Some time between the end of communion and now Damien died.

I sneak into the crowd as they make their way through the big wooden doors, trying to blend in and not be noticed. I make eye contact with the man in the robes for a second but look away. I'm not sure why.

I was watching her dance earlier today. She would usually have classes today, but since it was Christmas Eve, I guess they were cancelled but she still danced by herself. I didn't hide from her today. I didn't sneak into a dark corner and watch her from a distance like I usually do. I stood right in front of the window and watched the whole time. She still didn't notice me. She becomes so enraptured in what she's doing that I don't think she's conscious of anything besides herself. She becomes the flame just like I do, barely conscious of an existence besides herself and her movements.

I finally hid from her when she's done. I watched as she made her way home and up the apartment stairs to her husband. They kissed and sat around the Christmas tree opening each other's presents. I imagined her begging him to let her open them early, even though it wasn't quite Christmas. I stared at the lights that lined their tree and focused on them until the sounds of the traffic in the streets didn't exist and for a brief second, I felt like it was me that was in there and she was opening my gift.

I pulled out the box from under my coat. The box that held everything that was important to me. The box that I had been filling for the past year. The box that has been left on her doorstep on Christmas Eve every year for so long that I've lost count. The key is tied to it with a ribbon I found lying on the sidewalk. I walk up to her doorstep and ring her bell, leaving the box there for her to find. And just like every year, I walk away before she can see who it is that leaves them there for her. Then I walked to the church and met up with Damien, not knowing that it would be the last time I saw him.

I go home but can't sleep, knowing that tomorrow she'll dance to what I've left her in the box.

***

It's Christmas day and all the familiar faces and I gather around a fire that we've made in an alley and pass bottles of wine around and tell stories. I've told everyone that Damien died and the ones that knew him are sad but we try not to let it bother us. It's just something that you have to deal with. Every week someone starves, alone by themselves unable to find food or hustle enough money. This time of year is the worse because of the weather. You prepare yourself for it. You know that your friends are going drop off slowly, one by one, year by year, finally defeated by the cold winter nights.

Sally is running from one person to the next, telling them all about how she's going to be moving into her apartment soon. "I be livin' duh high life," she tells them. "Next Christmas we all be gettin' round my tree and I have presents for y'all. We cun drink dat egg nog 'n'eat us a feast. I'll git me wunna dem mistle toes maybe you can gimme a big ol' kiss, aye Harry?"

"Sure Sally," I say.

***

It isn't cold but it's snowing. The bright neon lights of the city are shut down because no one wants to be open on Christmas. Everyone has gone home to hibernate in the evening with their families. Everyone but her. I cut through an alleyway knowing that she'll be there in the dance studio. She'll know that I'll watch her but she won't see me.

She's there already when I peer from the dark corners of the surrounding building. The studio is brightly lit and I see her talking to the man that she always brings

8

with her. He's sitting at the piano in the corner of the room, explaining something to her on one of the pieces of notebook paper that I've left her. She's nodding her head in understanding, her curly blonde hair floating up and down.

The man puts my notebook on the piano and makes some notes here and there with a pencil. She dims the lights in the studio and poses in the middle of the room, waiting for the music, the music that I've written.

I see his hands begin to play the keys. Every night for the last year I've contemplated and obsessed over every note, trying to anticipate how the music will make her move. Even though I can't hear it with my ears, I hear it in my head. The soft beginning, with high pitched notes tinkling through room, and she moves in slow fluid movements, eyes closed, listening intently, improvising dance steps to the music.

The music swells and her arms and body begin to make circular motions through the air, her feet lifting off the ground for eternity and resting suddenly as she moves into a pose, held so briefly before twirling, her body wrestling with the beauty of centrifugal force.

In those moments when she dances to the music which I spent so long composing in the darkness alone, with only my imagination and obsession to keep me going, she becomes my candle. She hypnotizes me with her movements and the surrounding world and myself slowly drift away and there is only her. Only her movements and there are no thoughts. I'm not homeless. I'm not hungry. I'm not even me. I'm simply a pair of eyes, trapped in a snow globe, watching an angel dance for an eternity beneath snowy skies.

His hands are moving in rapid, almost jagged motions and I know that the climax of the song is here. Could these two hours have gone so fast? And next year seems so far away. Her body is jarring around in nearly violent advances, the sweat coursing over her face, her hair drenched and whipping around, and her eyes still closed, not opened once through the whole piece. And then they stop.

She stays in her pose long enough to look over at the man that played my song and he nods at her and she knows that it's over. She looks out the window for me like she does every year but won't see me. She leaves the studio and locks it and they walk down the street where she will go home and spend the rest of the night with her husband. I leave them alone on Christmas because he's shared her with me long enough for tonight.

Before she leaves, she leans down to the ground and puts the empty box next to the door. When she is far enough out of sight I pick it up. It's empty like it is every year. Waiting to be filled with another song.

***

When I finally make it home, Sally is passed out in my corner, curled up in my blankets, the smell of wine permeating from her black skin. I think of Damien and for a second I'm scared to try and wake her, scared that I'll go to her and she won't be breathing but when footsteps get close to her she wakes up, eyes wide with inebriated exuberance, smiling that huge toothless smile.

"What took you so long shugga'?"

"Just something I had to do Sally."

"Awwwww… you watchin' dat pretty thang dance again aintcha'? Well, I found jew a lil' Christmas present," she says and pulls out a box from underneath the covers, wrapped in newspaper with a piece of twine around it for a bow.

"What is it?"

"You know you gotta open it ta find out."

I untie the twine and the newspaper fall off to the ground. It's inside a box that says carrots on it from, probably from outside some restaurant. I shake the box and it makes a tinkling noise that sounds high-pitched notes. I undo the flaps and look inside. It's a tiny toy piano that little kids have with little multi-colored keys that would fit their tiny fingers. I look over at Sally and she's still smiling but her eyes are closed and I know she's falling back asleep. "I seen dat," she says in an exhausted voice, "and thought to me, man… dat Harry always saying how he used to be sum big shot piano playa'. So's I grabbed dat from duh trash and got you a nice lil' package. I knew dat gonna make yo Christmas Harry, I just knew it. But now you gotta play me sumtin'."

And so I played part of the song I wrote and the notes sounded just like they did in my head. And as I played, I could hear Sally slowly drifting off to sleep and the last words I heard on Christmas was Sally saying, "We be livin' da high life soon Harry. Me an you baby." But somehow I already felt as though I was.

Untitled
Laura Lee Atherton

"I always wanted to see the inside of that house," I say. He just turns his back, gives his head a little shake, and moves away. "Perhaps if I wind myself around you, you'll wrap yourself around me?" I suggest. He chuckles. I'm waved off again. "But I really thought if I did everything just right, things would be how I'd imagined them- in the end."
He turns back toward me. The chuckling louder now, mocking. There's condescension in that tone so thick between and around us that I can barely squeak in a breath. "That house," he explains to me so carefully I may as well be his child, "is nothing like you'd want it to be". I don't tell him I know better. I don't explain that, whatever it is, it's what I wanted- I just wished to know. He desires for me to be the fool before I've even had the opportunity to prove it or not.
I smile coyly, put on that air of slight detachment, reel myself in as though I haven't been that transparent after all. Pick to "lose" this battle.
Sometimes They forget, most times actually, that I often let them have the illusion that They've won. It's just one house, after all. Not the whole village, island, or even the entire sea.
My smile grows brighter as my heart softens and truly opens up to him.
"Let's do that dance we do, the one you taught me," I finally reply. I let him take the lead through those intricate steps, but I know until the end of the song- and past- who's really leading, after all.

Sara 423

Michael Deaton

Warren arrives at the bookstore slash coffee shop and peers through its glass walls. He stands for a moment in his blue jeans and Abercrombie shirt, perusing the small cliques of youths mingling and socializing. Behind them a bulletin-board with fliers of upcoming concerts, 'for-sell' ads and a missing persons flier of a teen girl with long blond hair. "How eager they all seem." he thought to himself.

He sees the red hooded sweatshirt with the blue backpack setting alone on a stool in the periodicals section, thumbing through a teen magazine and drinking a berry flavored Snapple. Her blue jeans are rolled up showing just the very tops of her pink socks which are sheathed inside a pair of black canvas Converse gym shoes.

Warren approaches from behind and says, "Fancy meeting you here." She spins on her toes to face her chat room confidante`. She smiles and squeaks out, "Warren?" He smiles and she reaches out to embrace him as if they had been best friends forever. Through her cotton hooded top he can feel the firmness of her youth and the resolve of her ribcage affirms him of her slenderness. Warren is pleased.

They find a spot where they both can lounge for a moment and talk. A soft couch with a coffee table. His eyes are all over her shape as he watches her shift for a comfy position. "It's about time. I finally meet the infamous Sarah423 in the flesh." Warren proclaims with a smirk on his clean-shaven face. Sarah smiles back. "You're taller than I imagined, and your hair looks better in person." Sarah giggles and stretches her gum.

"Does my hair look that bad on the net?"

"Not exactly bad. It just looks thicker here where I can see you better."

Well, do you like it so far?"

"Do I like what I see, you mean?"

"Yeah."

Sarah stands slowly, her eyes locked on his crotch as she rises. "Tell you what. Let's get out of here and I'll let you know *exactly* what I think. That's unless you think I'm too young, of course?"

Warren rises himself. "Let's go"

On the way to his apartment, Sarah dances in her seat to music on the radio. Warren thinks to himself that this has never been so easy before. He grins and silently

celebrates his luck. He knew that he would get her eventually. He just had no idea it would be this easy. She was dumber than he had expected. He can barely contain himself watching her touching her own breasts. Moving her hands down to caress her own youthful thighs was almost too much for him.

Sarah turns down the radio. "Why don't you park the car back there somewhere?" His head quickly jerks in her direction. They are driving down a very private part of highway. All he had to do was find a dirt road to turn off onto that leads back behind the woods. He knew that it would be safe and no one would be able to see or hear anything from the road.

"This looks perfect!" he says to his young companion. "No one around for miles." Warren stops and kills the engine in a spot that's far from the highway. It has trees and bushes that would make a great place to hide a platoon of military tanks. "Do you have anything?" Sarah asks, smiling. "If not, I have something right here."

Warren wakes to find that he's been stripped naked and tied to a tree. Handcuffs bind his wrists and steel bicycle cables held together with a thick combination lock truss his ankles. He's completely immobile. Sweat drips from his

forehead. He's still somewhat dazed but conscious and, very much alive.

"Wha...what the fuck? What's happening?" he asks. The sound of confidence no longer in his voice. Sarah slowly turns her gaze towards him. "Ah, so you're finally awake. This is what put you to sleep." Sarah throws a personal stun gun at his feet. She walks towards him. She looks somehow different to Warren. The look of innocence he remembers from before has disappeared from her face. Standing only inches from his face now, Sarah peers into his eyes. "Playtime is over, lover. I think you're in big trouble."

"What?"

"You're not as smart as you think you are, Mr. Bercot." Sarah's back turned to him now.

"How do you know my last name? What kind of game...."

"Patty Keeler."

"Patt...who are you talking about?"

He watches as she goes to her back pack on the ground and pulls out a paper. She walks slowly back to him and shows him what she has in her hand is not just a piece of paper. It's a photograph of a girl. A young girl with blond

hair. "Patricia Keeler! She was my 13-year old sister, and you murdered her!"

His jaw drops to the floor and his blood red eyes open wide in disbelief. "No! I didn't do anything to her, I swear!" The metal from the handcuffs cutting into his skin as he struggles to free himself. "Don't try to deny it, you son of a bitch! I know the whole story. You're a pedophile that raped and murdered my little sister, and now you're going to die!"

"Please! I'm sick! I need help!"

13

"Beg."

"Wha..?"

"I said beg you coward! Beg like my sister begged when you killed her to death! Beg like all the girls you've killed!"

"Please…I beg you! Don't kill me!"

"I'm not going to kill you, Warren."

He looks up with spit and drool running from his mouth. "You're not going to kill me?"

"No, Warren. I won't kill you. But *they* will." Sarah grabs a glass jar from her back pack. The contents of which being a small sample of assassins.

Warren looks in horror. "Fire ants!" He knows Southern Texas is filled with them and what they can do to living flesh. He pleads and begs Sarah. She laughs as she wraps his head around the tree with duct tape. She then pours honey around his now weak and paling body. Sarah lets the twenty or so fire ants out of the jar and onto Warren's body, knowing that their pheromones will attract more fire ants.

Within an hour his body will be covered. Their stinging pincers sinking into his skin. Every bite will be one tiny piece of excruciating Hell. Much like the Hell she feels herself whenever she thinks of how she encouraged her little sister Patty to meet Warren in the first place. And how she never told anyone that she knew where Patty was headed the very last time she saw her.

Sarah gathers her things and walks to Warren's car. The memory of her sister is with her every step.

Bellowing Alleyway

Philip Kurut

The masterpieces of one generation become the
Masterpieces of the next for simple legacy.
On the coattails of the previous generation
Comes the next to preserve.
The next echoes for the sake of
Further preservation.
    For hope of immortality.

Blash

Philip Kurut

Drawing the line,
Breaking it clean,
And taking everyone with me.
Holding down the fort
And burning down
To rebuild the places forgotten.
Praying to a God I can't see
To reach a place I've never been.
Letting go of the past
To insure an unknown future.
Learning from mistakes
Hoping I'll never have to use the lesson.
Searching the soul
To lose myself for a moment.

Queen Macaroni

Philip Kurut

Boredom creeps into our minds when we are least
Aware.
Soon we are dazing off and thinking of
Nothing in particular.
Slipping into our daytime
Coma and awakening into our
Daydream.
Traveling out of ourselves,
But leaving nothing behind.
Temporary is the dream and comatose of the day,
But forever the dream plays on for us to escape.

THE TRINITY CITY
Darin Leinbach

Blues boys hangin', leather black with Chicago Midwest rasp passing circle on open jam night, talkin' all deys shit and never giving themselves enough props, under the crystal clear bottom half moon rainbow light pollution hanging over the Trinity City

Moe's fashionably serendipitous showings in claustrophobic amplified smoking booth sections with a boyfriend she talked drunk about last night, and now I know why they're here, I've had that talk here too, under the full moon rising between the haunted fall cityscape of the Trinity City

The impassioned ones, none who love their art more, protesting modern music media with their bands, their play-lists, playing musicians who've toured all over the world as well as outer space, and in between air time we lift off and turn on streaming straight to your sweater beneath a fingernail moon-finger held down over top to recharge a Trinity City night

Paper lick buzzes, crazies in the street, meditatively contemplating tricks, their next move, always inciting a riot, or at least a hike through the shadows of ancient cottonwoods-sweeping the flood plain of the Saint Mary's like a horror film but oh so humorous highlights brought up the next morning, an all star breakfast after an all star clouded, extra dark night, in the Trinity City

Real conversation with a sober drunk, always a new physical connection with which to cuddle gettin' the fix, unseasonably warm January days spent only outside walking or sitting with a beverage and smoke in hand twitching for the spring to release the after Christmas anxiety, just another night and day with a clear sky worth the country drive, in the land of the Trinity City

Railroad bridge treks across trails once laden with many tracks, now sad with souls who walk along just as they did one hundred years ago wishing the steam still rose and revealed to them a ride right through the railroad city-slickers, an everlasting land of reincarnated travelers, explorers, hobos holdin' down and headin' out of their everlasting home on summer mornings as the wildflowers colors brighten with the sunrise, in the Trinity City

Those random serendipitous occasions of seeing an ex-love for the first time post her breaking your heart, she knows and won't even look at you, won't even wave hello, all the while you were anxious for passion talk with a friend who never showed and so you left to find but came up short until you saw his car at the original restaurant on your way back home, but he's nowhere in sight even still, and when you look-that's when you see the girl, that's when you tweak, that's when you shake and nervously talk to the waitress, who now is your only relief, a long lost friend in this place of emotional pain on full moon weekends, the Trinity City

Brilliant when detoxed, but oh so often hedonistically ingesting their vices, oh so many brilliant minds bursting with potential but settling for brief highs, the pos will never bust because they're on our side, erasing all lines, in this game of one on none we'll decide someday to compete in a life of forfeiting fearful masses, showing up is all that is required in order to defeat, to inspire maybe, the will is philosophized and chased with home brew, brilliant minds brewing in the depths without daylight far bellow the streets of the Trinity City

Tis a reason why many leave and always return, trinity triangle, seeking beings to serve a purpose, I'm done denying the reason for why I'm still here, I'm done with my skepticism, for I am the answer, multiple choice kids, all of the above, we've risen and ready to now gather who've bruised from Shannon's punch and healed wise and willing to show their face, I'm ready *now*, the training's over, yet everlasting, now's the time for super human heroes who won't save but start a revolution soon to be read to children before bed who can't wait to awake once more to a beautiful morning, in the Trinity City

Socially Stunted:
When a Boy's Most Productive Years Are Interrupted by Illness and Isolation
Adam Bodnar

A child's life – aside from having fun and experiencing happiness – revolves around learning and growing. However, seemingly almost all children inquired about their opinion of school would claim to loathe every minute of it. From early on, they classically associate their attendance at school with nothing but homework and the incessant berating of authority figures telling them what to think, say, and do. Children realize little of the psychological and emotional benefits that result from their continuously attending school and their interacting with classmates until adulthood. Perhaps most would relish in the thought of endless amounts of free-time completely devoid of teachers' and classmates' predominance.

Typically, only involuntarily would an unfortunate minority know and feel the effects of these circumstances. Any number of illnesses in particular could potentially prevent a child from continuing his educational career within the school system indefinitely. When this happens, a child and his family feel devastated. Also, in these times when conventional parents both acquire and maintain full-time jobs, a sickly child would only have whatever few physically undemanding sources of immediately accessible entertainment he could find to keep him company. Consequently, a pre-teenaged boy will become infinitely susceptible to – along with mental illness in general – the developing of an absolutely hopeless and negative outlook on life once isolated for a prolonged and undisclosed amount of time.

The numerous diseases that could potentially bring about the perpetual isolation of a child quickly approach irrelevance in comparison to the subsequent emotional turmoil experienced. Especially if the nature and origin of an illness remains in question or if the ailment lacks a treatment or cure, the confusion and frustration of not knowing gradually and certainly exacerbates an already emergent depression.

Coupled with the confusion of an affliction's cause, fear of contagiousness prevents any interaction with (former) classmates from taking place. Just as another child might understandably fear contracting any disease, the sickly child would by no means desire taking the risk of passing illness onto his friends. Parents of the ailing would only prevent social interaction, seeing as how they would not wish their fate of caring for and grieving over an ill child on the parents of another.

Regardless of the fact that the contagiousness or lack thereof of a disease would Surely transpire, the few and far between visits made to an ailing child would only eventually occur out of compassion. Also, a sick boy who already views himself as utterly different and diseased in comparison to his healthy peers would probably succumb to an overwhelming feeling of jealousy after a friend's departure. These elements together – all the while unspoken and unconsciously – make further visits mutually implausible. The eventual lack of all interaction with other children causes the ailing boy to suffer an even further diminished self-worth, because all children depend upon their peers for approval and their ultimate self-perception (Evans 245-46).

All public schools offer home-bound programs for those children unable to attend school due to illness. Considering the individual attention, a tutor might spend an hour a day with an ailing child and easily accomplish the equivalent of what would take

18

place during one school day. An isolated child would come to revere that reliably consistent source of interaction and would probably spend much of his day looking forward to and preparing for it.

Together with an unstable mind, this newfound motivation provides an ultimately addictive circumstance. Already suffering from severe depression, this chemical imbalance makes an isolated boy all the more susceptible to obsessive behavior. Having essentially no other reason to wake up in the morning besides getting ready and anticipating a little attention, a child might feel compelled to perform certain actions with the intention to impress. Not only might the isolated boy perform to the best of his abilities with regards to whatever a tutor might assign, but with time abound – and for as much as his illness could physically allow – he might for instance clean neurotically. All the while believing his actions serve an honorable purpose, he unknowingly acquires and advocates the symptoms of obsessive compulsive disorder.

After attempting numerous times to return to school, countless melancholic doctors' appointments swiftly and doubtlessly emerge as the only time an ill and isolated child can spend away from home. Rather than possibly enjoying any time away from home, however, the sickly child would more likely feel tremendously anxious about it. After having thoroughly concluded that a child cannot attend school due to illness, that child becomes prone to whole-heartedly dreading the thought of others not taking him or his illness seriously. Consequently, the boy – already suffering the chemical imbalance due to depression – will begin to exhibit some symptoms of paranoid schizophrenia. Through fearing the act of someone associated with school – or at least his previous life – simply seeing him away from home, he might even go so far as to hide himself when leaving the house rather than enjoying the change of scenery.

Of all the doctor appointments the inexplicably sick child goes to, some doctors might assume that a sick and secluded child must feel depressed and try to recommend a psychiatrist. Lack of treatment for childhood depression leaves doctors with little options for its treatment, and the FDA consequently approves the use of antidepressant drugs ("Helping..." 111). Parents of the ailing child would reluctantly allow their child to take antidepressant drugs however, with the growing cases and warnings of some children becoming more prone to committing suicide only after they start taking the medications (Ringold 537-38).

By this time the admittance of any or all emotional anguish experienced seems only humiliating to a boy. Programmed from early on that boys do not cry or get upset, he will probably do much to hide his despair and anomalous thoughts from even those closest to him. All the while never desiring professional help or treatment, those most disturbed by such a plight only perpetuate their suffering by gradually expressing even less of their true feelings.

This vicious cycle created causes a sick child to experience severe depression without purpose. As opposed to feeling miserable because of an abundance of illness and isolation, one's depression will only increase ten-fold as he might find himself sad only for the fact that he feels sad. In addition, a boy feeling embarrassed of his depression becomes inclined to suffer from unimaginable hopelessness. If his every thought did not already relate back to suicide, having lived for months turned into years of isolation would almost guarantee it.

The parents of continuously ill and isolated children must realize as early as possible, that severe depression – as well as a high susceptibility to other mental illness – most likely plagues their children. No one could expect a child to admit their own mental illness and take the proper steps in treating it.

Anyone who grew up loathing school should realize all that it has done for them. The precious social interaction that comes from consistently attending school until adulthood not only teaches children how to deal with others, but it proves invaluable in ensuring their mental well-being.

Works Cited

Evans, Theora. *"A Multidimentional Assessment of Children with Chronic Physical Conditions." Health & Social Work 29.3 (2004): 245-46.*

"Helping Depressed Children." Nature 431.7005 (2004): 111.

Ringold, Sarah. *"Antidepressant Warning Focuses Attention on Unmet Need for Child Psychiatrists." JAMA: Journal of the American Medical Association 293.5 (2005): 537-38.*

there's no competition
Bryce Gustafson

there's a line drawn across this page
incorporation involves a fine divide
it's too much to rush into
now
but
against my better refinement
i follow and run
cancer is my song
and such is life
rattle on
rattle on
cheers
the love never ends
any moment
i
deem wrong.

must have TV
Bryce Gustafson

give me three hundred and sixty three channels on my cable TV.
give me desperate grey idols surviving forever on dvd
give me fast food commercials smothered in mashed potatoes, chicken, gravy, corn, and
cheese
give me pharmaceuticals i have to ask my doctor about so i can buy some relief
give me talking heads explaining the cure for dealing with social decease
give me news that will broaden my knowledge about the life of celebrity
give me reality where everyone is real and hasn't sold their dignity
give me a god whose hustlers are buying and selling eternity
give me money and i will show you everything you need
give me that remote so we can witness the new divinity

inspiration's a bitch
Bryce Gustafson

inspiration is a lady
who lives down the block
in a back alley of my mind
sometimes
i look out my window
to see her walking an imaginary pet
that i wish were me

Of Dust Bunnies
Jess Boldt

Tiny black bugs resembling periods in a small print book hovered around the sink. Every few seconds a particularly brave gnat would dive for the pile of soiled dishes, only to be hit by a current of Lysol. It then proceeded into a nosedive towards a mountain of porcelain plates and plastic utensils. A variety of encrusted sauces and dry particles of substances that may at one time been considered edible accented the china.

Scott Burshell looked down the blue cap of the spray can as if lining up the sights of a rifle. He squinted his left eye while keeping the right eye closed. Another insect flew in the path of his vision. Taking careful aim, he pressed down on the button. The pressure built in the tall aluminum can to release a small stream of sanitized air then nothing. He shook the can hard and tried his shot again. Nothing. With his free hand he brushed his sweat dampened, light brown hair out of his face. His bright green eyes stared intently at the Lysol. The can was adorned with an illustration of a spring meadow. Each blade of grass was gently brushed with dewdrops. The thick odor that hung in the air more resembled a hospital restroom than a lovely spring meadow. He resolved to retire for the night.

He dropped the aerosol can into the crowded sink. He exited the recessed kitchen of his studio apartment. The entrance to a closet sized restroom stood next to the kitchen. The main room was sparsely furnished. A few boxes of varying size littered the carpet. A brown futon rested on the far side of the room against white drywall. It was opened to the sleeping position where a small white sheet and pillow lay on top. At the foot of the futon was a colorful, multi fabric pile of clothes.

The wall opposite of the futon held the only window in the apartment. A small single panel setting that looked out onto a small brick courtyard that was surrounded by a massive garden of wilted wildflowers and green brown bushes. A large stonewall surrounded the garden and wrapped itself behind the carriage house. The only exit near the apartment was a wooden gate. Beyond the gate were alleyways and a large vacant factory that at one time produced locomotive parts for a local railroad company.

Opposite of the carriage house, across the courtyard, stood the back of a large brick manor. Attached to the first floor was a screened in patio. Above that rested the second floor. A shroud of Boston ivy clung to the brick, concealing any windows that may have been there.

Scott awoke abruptly in the night. His muscles stiffened as a shrill scream pierced through the window. He laid there in temporary paralysis. The second scream sounded as though it held itself at a distance then raced through the window. He jolted back against drywall. The agonizing voice cried out in constant repetition. He was too far to see anything that may have been outside. The screaming became constant as he managed to dig around the pile of clothes on floor and locate a pair of jeans. Staring wild-eyed at the window, he managed to put the pants on. He then dove into a pile of clothes. Crawling on the floor and past the cardboard boxes, he slowly made his way to the window.

Once there he raised his head to see what was outside. His body flung back towards the floor at each scream. "Must be an injured rabbit. Just a rabbit, nothing else," he said under his breath.

A few very deep breaths later he raised his head fully. It took a few moments for his eyes to adjust to the dark of the garden outside. In the courtyard he could make out what looked like a wheelchair that had been turned on its side. Next to it was a small humanoid figure squirming around the base.

Scott drew up to look closer. The shrill screams grew more desperate. He ran to the front door. Once outside he made his way through the garden until he came up to an old wooden chair with large metal wheels attached to the sides. A few feet away was a very elderly woman wearing a long white night shirt. She was crawling around the ground screaming uncontrollably.

"Oh my God. Hold on. I am going to get you back into your chair," he sputtered as he tipped the heavy chair onto its wheels.

The woman continued to scream as Scott wrapped his arms around her thin torso. She was incredibly light, making the task easy. She stopped screaming and adjusted herself in chair.

"Where's my seat pillow?" the old woman snapped sharply from underneath the long white hair that covered her face.

Scott went to knees and began inspect the ground. He quickly found the cushion and handed it to the woman. "Are you alright? What happened?" Scott asked in a gentle voice.

"Harold! Harold!" the woman shouted.

"I am over here dear," a shaky voice called from the darkness of the garden.

The skeleton like shadow of bent man emerged from the darkness of the garden. He hobbled over to the woman in the wheelchair. The old woman's arm darted out at Harold. She cried out as she held his hand tightly. With her other hand she rolled up his sleeve of his left arm. In the darkness Scott could make out small lacerations on the surface of his skin.

"I knew it. You have been in it again. Let me see your face," the woman scolded.

Harold leaned down, his back cracking in process. The woman took her fingers and began to massage the skin of his face. Silhouettes of thick black liquid dropped from her fingers. "Get inside right now. I almost killed myself looking for you."

The frail man slowly stood erect and began walking towards the patio of the main house. Scott stood there in confusion. The woman turned her head to the young man. She then wheeled up closer to him, her wooden chair creaking with each revolution of the large wheels.

"Is everything alright?" he asked nervously.

"You must be Mr. Burshell, our new tenet. I believe we talked over the phone. I see you got the key I sent you."

"I have. I trust you received the deposit and rent"

"What are you doing out here so late?"

"I... I heard you screaming. I wanted to see what was wrong. Actually I didn't know what was going on," he replied. "Edith, wasn't it?"

"Just keep to yourself and mind your own business. When your rent is due, just place it in the metal box attached to the patio. Don't bother coming in. You have no reason to," the woman stated with obvious venom. "Where are you working?"

"Actually. I just dropped out of college this spring. Had to get away for a bit. But I have plenty of money. I don't have a car and I took out the last of my school money. It's more than enough until I find something," he replied. "Are you sure he's okay?"

The woman reached out her hand. Her boney fingers wrapped around Scott's wrist. They felt cold and began to sting. "You just mind your business."

Scott stumbled backwards, breaking the frigid grip. He struggled to stay on his feet. Instantly a wave of nausea rushed over him. He took a few steps forward then backwards. The old woman sat completely still. He tried to walk towards his apartment. He only made it a couple of steps before his vision became blurred. At the last moment of consciousness he felt the back of his head hit the brick of the courtyard.

The heat of the sun pounded on his skin. He opened his eyes slowly, squinting at the bright sky above him. The next sensation he felt was a strong headache. Moving his head slightly to each side he realized that it rested on a pillow. He made a brief effort to get up from the brick courtyard.

"Hey there. Just stay down for a bit longer," a female voice instructed.

The voice had come from behind his head. Tilting his chin upward he saw the face of a young woman above him. Her brown hair was highlighted with red streaks. It was just long enough to tuck behind her ears with a few locks hanging in front of her soft facial features. Her tiny nose rested an inch above her mouth on a face that was dotted with small brown freckles. Her eyes were a blend of brown, gold and red.

"How much did you drink last night?" She placed her hand upon Scott's forehead.

"What?" Scott responded in a strained voice.

"Well, you were obviously drinking. Unless you just walk around stranger's gardens half naked at night sober. I guess you could be a pervert. Although that sounds completely reasonable, it still doesn't explain why you would throw the back of your head against the ground. Putting all the facts together, I cleverly deduced that you got drunk and passed out in my backyard."

"No, I live here."

"Um, no you don't. I've lived here all my life. Twenty-four years to be exact. Not once have I had the pleasure." The girl moved her eyes to one side and smiled coyly. "Unless you are some sort of creepy mole boy that has been living in my basement. Only coming up to the surface to steal other people's potato chips and whatnot."

Scott made another attempt to get up but quickly gave into gravity. "I am not a drunk and I am certainly not a, what was that? Mole boy. I live in the apartment back here," he stated.

The girl turned her head towards the apartment then looked back down. "When did you move in?"

"About a week ago. And I'm not a trespasser."

The girl stared at him intently. Her face looked almost forlorn for a moment. She shifted to Scott's side giving him a better view of her. She was slight in build and wore a loose sleeveless brown shirt with the face of a cartoonish blue rabbit listening to an oversized pair of headphones. "Oh. I'm sorry. I guess my grandmother didn't tell me she rented out the garage.

"Grandmother?" he repeated in a weak voice. "That's why I was out here. She fell in her chair. I think she was looking for your grandfather. It's foggy. I can't remember it all. But I don't think I am welcome here."

"Yeah, that's my grandmother. Just pay your rent on time and she won't mind you. They're really old. Don't pay her too much attention."

"And you are?"

"My name is Amanda," she stated and started to smile.

"What's your name sir?"

"Scott."

"Scott, I think it is time we got you inside. I would have carried you but you were pretty much dead weight. And I had no idea where to take you. But I guess I know where to take you now. You have to help me out here. I am still not carrying you."

Amanda wrapped her arms around Scott's chest. She took notice of his weakness and shifted her arms lower. She helped him prop himself up to a sitting position. The two shuffled to their feet, Scott leaning on Amanda like a crutch. They slowly made there way to the front door of the small carriage house. He opened the door and the two of them went inside.

"Just help me to the bed. I will be fine after awhile."

"You said you have been here for a week?" Amanda asked while helping Scott dodge the various boxes.

Once the two reached the sweat stained futon, she gently helped him to a horizontal position. She then began to walk through the main room of the studio apartment until she came to the recessed kitchen.

"I am still not sure how you hit your head. I don't see any bottles or cans about so I am bit more inclined to believe that you weren't drinking."

Scott struggled to recall the exact details of the night. Brief images of a wheelchair and the sense memory of cold remained. "I remember helping your grandmother up. There was some yelling, at Harold I think."

"Christ, it looks like you have been here for more than a week. Look at the amount of dishes you built up."

"I just can't remember all of it. But I know what I would feel like if I drank enough to crash outside. I feel like shit, but I'm not hungover."

"Would you be insulted if I did your dishes?" Amanda asked.

"I think you've helped me enough. I'll get around to it at some point."

"It would make me feel better. I guess I'm just like that. Would you be insulted?" she asked.

"No, knock yourself out."

Amanda began to pull the dishes from the sink. She stacked them according to size in a vacant spot adjacent to the sink. She then looked through the various white drawers until finding a half empty bottle of dish soap. After plugging the sink she began to run the hot water. She labored tediously over the steam, which mingled with the scent of neglected dishes. After some time she glanced over at the exhausted man.

"You must have tripped over a bush or something. It can get pretty dark out there. By the way, why would you want to move to a neighborhood like this? It's pretty run down."

"I know but the price was right. Besides, the outside doesn't seem to exist here. Were you really angry when you found me."

"Not really." Amanda stated without emotion. She placed the last dish onto the stack and walked towards the door.

"Hey. Are you taking off?" Scott asked.

"Yes. I should get back. I think you will be alright."

"What are you doing tomorrow?"

"What?"

"Well. I guess I would just like to hang out. Get to know you."

"Forget it. No big deal," she replied.

"Regardless. I would like to see you again. I don't know anyone around here and I've been getting kind of stir crazy. Would you meet me in the courtyard tomorrow?"

"What time?" she asked.

"How does twoish sound?"

"That could work. Get some rest. I guess. I will see you tomorrow." She walked out of the apartment, closing the door behind her.

The grey light of morning sulked from the window across the room. The day felt cooler than the previous day which made the surface of the futon much more comfortable. He sat up after sometime, his eyes fixed in a minor daze.

On his way back from the closet restroom his bare foot slammed into the side one of the cardboard boxes. Silently he bent over and opened it, revealing dusty contents of photographs, books, CDs, and various other objects. By 1p.m. the apartment had been transformed into a vibrant living space. Even the futon looked more inviting with a matching sheet set and pillowcases.

He put on a clean pair of jeans and blue t-shirt after grooming himself and made to leave. Upon opening the door a rush of chill air entered the apartment. Slightly confused he shut the door and went back to the folded pile of clothes. He put on a brown loose fitting sweater before exiting.

Sitting on long stone bench next to a patch of purple Foxglove was Amanda. A small maple tree was canopied above her head. The leaves were thick and green. Her hands were hidden in the long sleeves of a dark red hoodie. Her blue Keds were kicking small clouds of dirt over the brick laid ground as her jeans swished around her legs. Scott stood there for a moment before walking over to her.

"Hey," he called pensively.

She stopped kicking her feet and looked up at Scott. "Hey you. Are you feeling better? You still look a bit out of it," she remarked.

He searched for the words for a few seconds then sat two feet from her on the stone bench. "Yeah, I think I'm feeling better. A lot better actually. Just in a bit of a fog. I can't remember any of them, but have you ever woken up knowing that you had strange dreams? And you just couldn't shake whatever feeling they gave you?"

Amanda smirked. "You do know why that is, don't you?"

"Why I feel like I haven't woken up from something I don't even remember?"

"Exactly. Look up at the sky."

Scott looked at the sky to see a blanket of grey clouds move slowly across it. "The weather?" he asked.

"Sort of. Where do you think your dreams go when you wake up?"

"Huh?"

"Well, they have to go somewhere. Most of them rush up to the sky and spread themselves across the universe. They embed themselves in time and space. A sort of memory bank I guess. However, when it is cloudy like today, they bounce off the clouds and back to where they came from. If it stays cloudy, then it's kind of like you have a chance to capture eternity. You can't always remember them because the air will strip away everything but the bare emotions that created them. So yeah, that's why you are out of it today," she stated quite assuredly.

"I never thought of it like that. I guess I never really gave dreams much thought. Still, it's worth putting logic aside. I think I like your explanation much better."

Their conversation continued for hours. Scott would tell the girl about his childhood, his days in college and everything in between. Each time he spoke, his memories would play clearer than they ever had in the past. By recalling his memories, he was reliving them.

He saw himself as a young boy. The boy sat on the curb at corner of a street lined with small houses and talk oak trees. The yellow school bus coming towards him as his stomach turned with nervousness. He saw himself at five, fourteen, then eight in the course of a few short recollections. He saw his first kiss and him sitting alone half way through his first school dance. After relaying one memory he would stop and ask her to tell him something about herself. She would smile softly. She would move a bit closer and ask him to talk for a little bit longer. Each scene passed without regard to chronological order.

A crisp wind swept through the floor of the garden, creating more clouds of dirt that rose in the air and past their faces. Amanda squinted her eyes and turned away from the assault. Scott finished the most recent recollection. He closed the few inches of gap that remained between them.

"Funny weather, huh?

Amanda turned back towards him and wiped her eyes with the red sleeves of her sweater. "Why's that?" she asked.

"Its June?" He paused. "And I guess it's just…"

Feeling the girl's hand push over his emboldened him just enough to lean in and close his eyes. The first kiss was short and barley made contact. The two moved an inch away, gently laughing. A brief exhale then they embraced with intention.

Scott brushed his hands through her hair, his fingers making momentary paths through the strands. His fingers contacted a fragile obstruction, then another. They crinkled and crushed underneath the slightest pressure. He pulled back to see leaves falling from the tree above them. Autumn leaves, golden reds and browns of all shades, each leaf picking up another hue from her eyes.

Confused, he kept brushing more of the leaves from her head. Amanda's eyes dropped, her expression darkened. "I'm sorry. I couldn't help it," she stated shyly.

"What? Are you saying that you…?"

"I'm sorry."

Scott looked around in amazement as dead leaves drifted from the small tree. Amanda reached her arms around his torso and began to sob softly. Her red sweater could barely conceal that her body had begun to shiver. He wrapped his arms around her shoulders then placed his right hand through her hair again.

"It's okay. It's the most beautiful thing I have ever seen," he assured her gently. They kissed, gathering falling leaves until the tree was shed bare.

***

Weeks passed in the garden. Each morning the leaves would bud on the maple tree. Each afternoon Scott and Amanda would meet underneath it. By evening the leaves would loose their chlorophyll and drift down on the embracing couple. He would tell her about memories that he thought were long forgotten until one day he could recall nothing more.

"It's odd. But I think you have just heard my entire life story. Well, at least up until when I moved here." He brushed her hair away from her autumn eyes. "I feel really selfish. I really don't know anything about where you came from. Other than you live with your grandparents inside that house," he stated, pointing to the large brick structure.

"I would really like to see your apartment."

"Okay but..."

"I would really like to go to your apartment."

The pair walked through the door that led into the pristine studio apartment. Scott brought Amanda gently against the wall.

"It looks nice," she remarked before they locked themselves into heavy breathing and patient exploration. Every movement lent itself to a new sensation. Their clothes were removed before they collapsed onto the futon.

Scott woke up in the middle of the night. The crisp air circulated through the room. He pulled the comforter over the girl and closed his eyes.

The next morning met him with an empty bed. He stood and gathered his clothes from the floor. Amanda left no trace. He dressed and went outside. The grey sky contained a great feeling of joy for him. This feeling was enhanced after seeing Amanda sitting on the bench in the courtyard. He waved to her. She sprung up and ran to him.

"I didn't want to wake you up. I hope you slept well," she said as she wrapped her arms around him.

"I feel really good. Have you been waiting for me out here this whole time?" he asked.

"Well," she laughed. "Yeah, pretty much." She kissed him softly on the lips then grabbed his right hand with both of hers. She led him to the bench and sat down.

"What are you doing today? I have to run to the grocery later. I've got next to nothing left. I was thinking that we could get some dinner or something."

Her head tilted to the side. "I thought we could stay here today. Maybe we could find some more memories you forgot to tell me about. Or I could just listen to some more of the same again. I'm really not much for leaving."

"I would love to, but I can't stay here everyday. I'm going to have to get a job at some point. I was actually thinking about signing up for a few classes. For the fall, well the real fall at least," he said while pushing his fingers through her hair.

"This is real." Her eyes narrowed as her head shook, removing Scott's hand.

"This is better than real. And I could stay here forever. But…"

"But what? How can this not be real? It's here. You can see it. Don't you like it what I have given you. I gave you everything and now you are going to act like this. What's going on? Why did we…? You can't do this," she panicked.

"Do what? I am not going anywhere. I don't want to leave you if that's what you are afraid of. This is the best thing that has ever happened to me. Look. I will stay here for the day if you want. We can always go out later," he stated, hoping to calm her.

"I'm not going anywhere. This is the deal you made with me," she stated. Hot tears ran down her flustered face.

"What deal?"

"You don't understand anything. I can't leave here. This is all I have. I'm safe here. I thought I was safe last night. But if you leave…" she began to sob heavily.

"What's keeping you here? Whatever it is, we can get away from it. I can help you. If it's inside that house, I will go inside and do whatever needs to be done. But you have to let me in there."

Amanda stood up hastily. She stammered for words as she stared at Scott who was sitting confused on the stone bench. Her mouth inhaled, making a brief yelp before her body turned to run.

Scott watched as she ran to the side of the manor's patio. He stood up and followed her to the house. A vague familiarity washed over him as came near the patio. He stumbled around. His knees dropped to the hard red brick below him. He bit his lip hard to maintain consciousness. Belts of nausea continued until he managed to crawl several yards away from the house. He sat there catching his breath, unable to rise to his feet.

The screen door from the side of the patio swung open. "Amanda."

The figure of a frail man stepped out of the door and walked towards Scott. It was Harold. His pace was slow but each step was determined. Harold reached out his withered arm. Scott grabbed it and was pulled to his feet. The young man leaned on the elderly savior.

"It's alright. Let's get you away from here," Harold stated with kindness.

Harold led Scott the stone bench. The young man was still breathing heavily. His face had become pale.

"Settle down. You'll be alright soon," the elderly man stated.

"I… I have to talk to Amanda. How do I get back in?"

"When you are ready to make your decision I suppose. But don't take that lightly. It's going to be a very tough decision to make."

"What decision?" the boy asked.

The concern in Harold's eyes changed to a daydream expression. "You don't have any whiskey in your apartment, do you?"

"What?"

"You see, Edith always puts a bottle just out of reach. I sometimes manage to get some, but it's quite painful. Believe me." Harold's eyes grew wide and lit up. "The

30

only thing I really remember well is drinking good whiskey with my buddies during the war. Each time it seemed like there were less and less of us drinking. But we always drank a bit for the one's who couldn't enjoy it with us? And we were particularly glad we were able to enjoy it ourselves."

Scott was confused. His body made several quick jerks as if it wanted to run to the house despite his state. He then noticed the distant look on the aged and cracked face of Harold.

"Why does she hide the bottle? Why would she just not get rid of it?" he asked.

"We had a daughter once. Now we have Amanda. That is how life works. I guess she couldn't let her go. I didn't mind staying at first, but now I just want to see my old friends again. Maybe have a few shots with them."

"HAROLD!" The shrill voice came from the patio. Harold stood up and made his way towards the large brick house.

Scott used all of his strength to rise to his feet. He inched towards his apartment, each step was excruciating. Finally he entered the small room. He collapsed on the futon, exhausted and defeated.

The hours passed. He laid on the futon, staring at manor through the window across the room. He hadn't noticed that dust had begun to gather on the ceiling above him. In an hour the entire surface was covered in a thick layer of grey dirt. Clumps of the dust began to rain onto the apartment below. In two hours he was completely covered by the substance. His only movement was to wipe the particles away from his face, clearing the obstruction to his view of the window.

This continued for a few more hours. He would cough harshly as his lungs desperately tried to clear the dust. From the kitchen and almost impossible to notice, came a tiny insect. It was about the size of a period from a small print book. It buzzed around the apartment, dodging the clumps of dust that rained from the ceiling with precision. Scott watched the tiny bug with admiration.

He sat up. Large balls of grey soot dropped from his body. He made his way through the shower of thick dust. His feet drudged through the sod and filth. His legs strained from the resistance, movement was measured in centimeters. He finally buckled a few feet from the door. He slumped into the mess, crawling through it until he finally reached the door. It was near impossible to breath anything but the dirt. His hand punched through the surface, fingers stretching out like tiny probes. This right index finally touched the bottom of the doorknob and alerted the rest of the digits. He turned the handle. An avalanche of grey dust cascaded from the door, sweeping Scott outside.

The blanket of grey sky had given way to the blue light of summer. He stood up, brushing off what he could of the dust that clung to his brown sweater. Perspiration condensed on Scott's body immediately. Towering over the landscape of green vegetation drenched with sharp yellow sunlight stood the brick manor. His feet moved, one after the other towards the house. He left a trail of thick grey dust behind him.

The heat reflected off of the brick. The walk grew increasingly tedious. Scott removed the loose fitting brown sweater, revealing a dark red t-shirt underneath. Leaving the garment on the stone bench that sat underneath the green leaves of the small maple tree, he continued his journey to the patio. He had made his decision and had not felt the slightest hint of nausea or fear.

The black mesh screen was impossible to see through. He walked around to the side where the screen door hung slightly off hinge. White chips of paint hung from the rotting wooden frame. Opening the door carefully, he stepped inside. It took a few moments for his eyes to adjust to the dim lighting. On the side opposite of the screen sat rows of shelves. On each shelf rested planting pots of various sizes, each growing different flowers, plants, and vines. Thousands of thick green caterpillars crawled over each plant. A symphony of terrible clicking noises echoed in the enclosure. Each worm tore food into their mouths with their large pointed mandibles. Across from Scott sat a small wooden table with a glass in the middle. Harold sat in a chair behind it. He stared at the empty glass, tears rolling down the time worn face.

"I'm in trouble," the old man moaned softly.

"I know," Scott whispered. "I need to see Amanda."

The old man brought his head up to look at the Scott. He smiled briefly, his eyes still wet with tears. "You're a good boy. But you shouldn't be here. I would leave if I could. But I am not allowed to. I used to be able to get around and…"

"Where did she put the whiskey?"

The old man brought his shaking arm from underneath the table. His thin finger stretched and pointed to one of the shelves of plants. "Between the tomato plants," he stated. "It's no use. No use at all."

The young man closed his eyes and nodded in affirmation. Taking a deep breath he went over and reached for the bottle with his right arm. A legion of the caterpillars crawled around his arm instantly. They began to feed, tearing away at the flesh. He reached further until his hand scraped a glass bottle. He pulled the bottle out quickly, his arm was covered the crimson of blood.

Scrapping away the last of the caterpillars Scott went over to the table. He poured the bottle into the glass until it was full. The old man wrapped his hand around the glass and smiled.

"I should never had stayed so long," Harold stated, raising the glass to his mouth. He drank the contents as Scott stood still, his arm still bleeding. The man placed the empty glass on the table. "So long dear boy."

Scott tried to say something but could barely breath. Harold's face began to sag and drip like warm wax. The skin on his forehead descended over his eyes. Instead of muscle and skull, there was only putty underneath. It drained from his sleeves as his body sunk in the chair. The putty collected on the ground and dripped through the cracks of the wooden floorboards. This continued until all that remained of Harold were a pair dusty brown slacks and a grey oxford shirt.

Wiping away the moisture from his eyes, he opened the door that led inside a large kitchen. An old wood stove sat in the corner of the near vacant room. A gentle heat radiated from the iron box. Next to the stove was the entrance to a large corridor. He continued past the kitchen and into the hallway.

On the walls were a series of antique pictures. He recognized a younger Harold and Edith in one of the first photographs. It was a wedding picture of them cutting a cake together as they smiled. As he continued through the corridor, the story of a young couple separated by war and then brought back together unfolded. He saw a photograph capturing the birth of their daughter. He watched as each picture captured the constant progression of time. The couple grew older in each snapshot. The daughter grew and had a child of her own.

The corridor opened up to a large foyer. It was ordained with vertical oak beams, which were ornately carved with images of grapevines reaching up to the ceiling that met angels, which had been carved into the rafters. Above was entrance was an enormous winding staircase that led a few feet away from large wooden door at the end of the room.

"You are not supposed to be here. What did you do?" Edith shouted. Her face twisted with frustration as she stared at Scott's right arm covered in small wounds. "What did you do, you wicked boy?" the woman shouted from her wheel chair.

"I just let him leave. He was very tired,"

The old woman shrieked loudly. The temperature of the room dropped instantly, causing frozen vapor to cloud from her mouth. The wooden rafters creaked as they adjusted to the cold. She placed her hands on the wheels of the wooden chair and began to move towards Scott rapidly. She grabbed his arm and clamped down hard with frigid fingers. Her body shook with malice as her grasp began to reopen the wounds.

Scott stood over her motionless. "I am sorry. You were always scared of losing people. Did you ever really enjoy the time you were able to spend with them?" He paused. "I guess I'm the biggest sort of hypocrite."

The frail woman looked at the young man's face. She stared in his eyes for a moment then loosened her grip. She brought her hand to her lap. "Was he...?" She began to sob softly. "I just thought I could keep him. I never wanted him to resent that. We used to walk in the garden. We planted everything ourselves. Then there was the damn war. Our sweet daughter, she was so beautiful. No one should have to die. And they didn't have to. I made sure of that. I did it because..."

Scott rested his damaged hand on the woman's shoulder. She shrugged her shoulders back.

The woman placed her hands on the wheels of the wooden chair. She positioned herself away from Scott and moved down the corridor that led to patio. Scott didn't turn around to look. He walked to the main door and placed his hands on the brass handle. He could hear footsteps coming down the staircase.

"Are you leaving or are you staying?"

Turning around, he saw Amanda standing on the staircase above him. A few stray strands of hair hung over her face. She was wearing a light blue summer dress that draped a few inched above her knees. She was clutching a picture frame in her arms. She had stopped mid way down the stairs.

"I wanted to talk to you. I was going to stay. I came to tell you that I was going to accept your deal. Then I realized it wasn't a deal but an ultimatum. Even then I wanted to stay." Scott stood there, his hair darkened and flat from perspiration. Wet grey dust covered every inch of his person. "He was right. Your grandfather was right."

"About what?"

"This is tough." Scott stood there, barley breathing. "I have to go."

"We don't have to be like... What about your apartment? What about your stuff?"

"Dust bunnies," he responded. "You don't have to stay here anymore. There really are good things outside. It may not be like autumn in the garden, but it can be pretty nice sometimes."

"You mean come with you?"

"Come with me. Go by yourself. I can't make you do anything. I don't know. Maybe it really isn't that great out there." He paused for a moment. "But this can't last forever. What happens when you use up the all the memories? What will you become? I have a good idea what may become of me. I won't..." Scott began to weep.

She choked back her tears then started down the stairs. Her face brightened as she smiled. Scott smiled in turn. Her face dimmed suddenly. She clenched the picture frame tight to her chest. She froze. "I will just find someone with new memories I guess."

Scott turned around and opened the front door. He stepped out into the warm August night. He found himself on a worn wooden porch that creaked underneath his weight. Panic streaked through him as he went to turn around. The door closed then latched with a deafening mechanical click.

The neighborhood was a stark contrast to the quiet of the garden. Condemned buildings lined the street. A few people milled around like drunken ghosts over cracked pavement.

Scott walked down hill that the house sat on. He came to the street below. Four white police cars raced past him, their sirens loud and piercing. He watched as the red and blue lights disappeared into the distance. After the street had become still again he moved in the same direction.

"Any change?" Scott looked through the blur of his vision. He saw a man in a dirty white t-shirt leaning against the wall of a liquor store. He wiped his eyes clear. The salt of his tears stung the wounds of his arm. Scott shook his head.

A crisp wind drew in from the ground. Two dead leaves floated with the current then stopped at Scott's feet. A second gust came through, picking up the leaves, moving them against his face. They hovered there for the briefest of moments before disappearing into the atmosphere above.

"Damn. It's getting cold early this year. I don't have time to get down to Florida. Don't you have at least a few bucks for a bus ticket?" the vagrant barked.

Scott exhaled. His mouth gave way to a slight smile. The lights of the liquor store went dark. He walked down the sidewalk, illuminated by the orange light from streetlamps overhead.

Life is Like a Cigarette
Michael Deaton

Pack them first
Conception.
Light up
Birth
Watch it burn
Every drag is another day.
Hold it a second.
Then exhale.
Half gone
Middle age.
Look to see how much is left
Memories.
Listen to the crackle; smoke fills the air
affecting others
Fruits of your labor.
One drag left
Final breath.
The flame is gone
Death.
Filter-corpse; ashtray-coffin.

Throw Your Vote Away
Brian Landrum

"Can a burned out sixties slacker pothead make a difference in the modern world? You may be surprised by this, but the answer is no." - Mike Zoss productions

Aside from the bed, the penthouse was spotless but too bright for the occasion, and after a while I started to wonder if anyone might have shared my dunce sense of analogies. The death shrouds made matters worse; my imagination only gained focus as I retained the image of a pale stabbed stomach in my mind alongside a stack of hotcakes with a dollup of butter melting away from top dead center. But without question the punctured stomach remained in true form under the bulkiest olive green tarp, and all I could do for the moment was stare at the plush opal carpet waiting on my eyes to ease out the illusory heat and light glaring through the east bay window.

"dead for approximately thirteen hours" the sketch report had read. Internal bleeding, severe organ damage, even spinal cord damage all from what appeared to be one blow with one sharp object, a blow likely hammered down intoxicated in dim lighting. This guy never saw it coming I thought. He probably never even had time to realize what had happened. Just a shocking stick and a gasp and it was all over.

I stood there with some notecards and one compact disc. I had three contacts for this mess and only one was good. I remembered the good one mentioning something about a song titled "Rockin' In the Free World" and assumed this would be the only source I needed to speak with. This one ought to be fairly uncomplicated I had thought, the thought had passed my mind just before I watched a black clamp slide in freezing time from the bed of the white Ford pickup ahead of my front bumper. One well-placed puncture in transit and my right front tire slumped alongside the stomach. My only spare was already on the left, so I ground the flat's rim in livid defiance of stupid chance, destroying it further for over three miles until I veered into the closest semblance of a repair shop.

The world of lesser punctures, Big Eaz-E Tire & Brakes in the free world. Time to play angry. I stared at the concrete floor and thought I don't think I can handle this much classic rock, hearing through the door the team of four maybe certified technicians bent to change two front tires on my truck right after one more vaguely founded thirty minute break. The foamy stained black FM radio speaker cracked out another blase extended guitar jam and I knew I should have made the two mile walk back for some catfish and garlic potatoes somewhere with good lighting. Trial and error I thought, supply and demand. Maybe I should apply for a job at this dump.

Their conversation tremored along: This guy says he only tried crack once and now he's biding his time, waiting for word from the overnight package handlers. He says these rumors of men losing hands and feet in forklift mishaps are unfounded, and he's probably right at least in a short sense. This is the F--- Municipal Airport for hang gliders and model airplanes, not a Civil War documentary.

But the methadone addict muffled to my left insists he heard some old man lost his very testicles in a freak freight conveyor glitch. And the fried chicken to my right supports this story, adding his own rendition of a hand lost in a snowblower. Autumn rain begins to plunk down on the tin roof. I left home for this? The middle-aged detail boy wants to go home. Go let your car warm up for 25 minutes. It's running rich. Just eat your microwavable cheeseburger.

After ten bad minutes number four asks if crack tastes like salt, but MGR can't remember. He's here, what more could a person want? 162 minutes until the next chance to sell a set of encyclopedias along with your oil change, ma'am, and the man is in charge that's for certain. The detail boy can leave if he promises to stay gone I thought, this wouldn't be a bad managerial position to hold if it were a one man shop.

But after twenty bad minutes the woman bumped through the purple metal door with a hard aluminum cane. The answer to my one phone call, she'd gone out of her way and we were alone in the concrete but she waved and told me not to worry about it. "I know how these clowns work," she said. "One of 'em is my stepbrother's son and he ought to know better. I wish they'd get a real shop around here somewhere."

She moved carefully into a yellow plastic chair and used another to elevate her feet. She opened a drink, stowed away the cane, then continued regarding her relation. "He's just like his dad," she said. "It shouldn't surprise anyone he is the way he is. I remember B-- used to pull the same kinda crap, standing around acting like he works harder than everyone else and he doesn't do a thing."

This poor woman could barely walk I thought, the product of pharmacuticals forging blind, but she endured nonetheless like an insect buried and burned and broken yet never destroyed, somehow more bound to life than any altruistic torturer could possibly perceive. I offered half of my candy bar and she took it.

With an eager bite she heard the technicians walk by away from the work and she shook her head until unloading a mock pistol made of two fingers and a thumb into the side of her head with a defiant chuckle. "There he goes with his buddies," she half-whispered. "It's like my grandma used to say: If Jesus Christ showed up at his front door and handed him a check for ten million dollars, he'd still drag his ass and find a reason to bitch."

Despite such bizarre short notice due to unexpected futility and the speaker's current imposition of what sounded like an undying beer commercial, she relayed her encounter with three women at an appliance store on the northeast side of Indianapolis: Three women laughing in a small circle before two hundred identical faces of Neil Young blaring on an encompassing wall of upscale television sets. Grey flimsy professional attire, tightly wound hair, dark thick lipstick and brassy spectacles all bobbed together

37

within a sea of simultaneous broadcasts, some weird guy sweating under floodlights in an outdoor arena.

She had been looking for a toaster and thought they worked at the place. 9:29 pm, she said. That was all I really needed. There were a thousand clocks in the place she said, and she was certain of the time. The women had balked at her request for help, but she said it was hard not to hear what they were talking about: The plutocrat vote the Reverend Doctor Mister Jackson Beam, the charming county councilman then running for mayor, the sure thing the great hope of tomorrow who would be found the next morning in a penthouse suite stabbed down and long dead.

Dead for approximately thirteen hours at 8:41am, nearly thirteen hours after this woman's encounter with a pack of Beam's esteemed collegues at any given appliance store. Twelve minutes to give. She said she heard them mention Beam by name. She said they spoke of the upcoming rally as if they worked for his campaign, that they seemed somehow enchanted by the guy on the other side of town who at the time likely stood opposite a mirror, preparing for cocktails in the shadow of death.

I thanked my source and walked her out past the stale panelled change counter to her old green sedan. She wished me well through the driver window and wrestled the oversized wheel to turn and pull away. The rims cranked and her left front fender popped, a fender buckled up to create the slight image of a fang arcing over the tire; the warped fender quivered like some kind of crushed serpent as the faded sedan rattled into the dim raining early evening.

I walked back to search for anyone, hoping begging for anyone to do anything so I could just leave. Just staple the rims on I thought, I'll work something out later. Just get me out of here. I watched a guy kneel down to look at something just beyond the jack holding the front of my truck minus front wheels in the air like a fake shark. He crouched in confusion, lost or abandoned and bored, content to crouch and maybe chuckle in resigned hesitation. My search produced little more from these who would now dictate my fate, so eventually in careful submission I found myself again in the company of FM Radio the sole companion. I should just make something up and phone in the demise of the Rev. Dr. Mr. Jackson Beam before it all unravels I thought, I may be foreordained to die before my triumphal exit from this concrete aquarium.

But I had no clue. Were there truly no random shady scumbags involved? It was as if God had simply employed an invisisble almighty cordless drill to stake a hole through the fleshy gut of this manicured man. I fantasized about an article titled "Mama Should Have Named Him Hubris", but there seemed to be no tragic flaws in sight, no one could even frame the guy, some hooker tried once but even she was just a pawn who decided to cash in and got caught. Wanda, I believe, was her name. She was in on a frame somehow, paid to present the appearance of lewd infidelity by latching on to Beam in public. She'd been paid by some long gone scam artist but took a fall when she tried to play the spouses against one another. Wanda Down On The Street told Beam's wife she'd take a hike for double the husband's final offer just before her ashen remains found final rest in City

Waste Disposal Dumpster #206.

And that was it. There were four people with access to Beam at the point of no return.
His wife said she was in the shower, and the three desk ladies were shopping for
appliances. So it all led back to the wife, she was it even though her polygraph passed
and Beam had carried all evidence into the grave. The foamy riffs kept coming below
vocals more irritating than interesting, just whining bitching about the oblivion of travel
and manipulative women. I thought of the edge submerged in Beam's abdomen amidst
the speaker's broadcast wailing, the dead man himself an endless ageless stone now
molded around the blade in grey steel shadows, and I watched the ages pass as mildew
and moss took root from nothing and crawled in a dim single cylinder of light to swallow
both the memory of life and the memory of murder, the mildew and moss giving birth to
small stringy dark stems erupting into great masses of green. And the light multiplied
and the green grew deeper until the growth twisted under and began to choke its very
foundation. The light burned brighter and the thicket began to rot under the steam, the
rotting the basis of fire hatching and heaving, stumbling about into a rage, a vortex now
screaming upon nothing but a surface, the rock and the blade both glowing red then blue
then white until reduced and concentrated to the same fleeting atmosphere which would
ultimately by negation destroy the fire itself. And through the emptiness I looked and I
saw the new and reigning trinity of white collar women lifted above the draped and
bloody American flag, and below Beam's wife, her perfectly trimmed black bangs and
pursed plum stiff lips, her flash white apron tied nicely, holding ready in one hand the
butcher knife smattered with blood.

My truck slammed down with only one front end wheel attached. Service technicians
scattered and snickered except one chosen, one who stood delayed next to the heap
screaming playful obscenities. I haven't heard a song by this band in at least twenty
minutes I thought, I have been trapped behind chicken wire windows to contemplate the
severity of political posturing. I wondered about peculiar eagerness, and the fabrication
of testimony was my best guess. The desk girls took him out one way or another, but
Beam was beside the point. They directed their hatred toward the real power, the boss;
the great Reverend Doctor had always been her pawn and they had played right along.
They toyed him into hiring them as a publicity stunt, but even then they took orders from
her. The wife and the desk girls simply postured this joke of a powerful man against one
another until it became evident the pawn must be destroyed alongside the opposition. So
with youth and numbers they struck first by the council and design of a volunteered sage,
they killed her indirectly, they caged in the spouses and killed him at the only time she
had no hard proof of innocence.

I watched my truck waver on three legs while the chosen one with cracked goggles and
thinning black hair wiped down his greasy toolbox with a stained maroon rag. He cursed
and spat and giggled. I studied this man's expectant defiant glares in my direction and his
position on the transcendental shitlist became quite clear. Up the road his father's
stepsister pulled onto the interstate, her beaten green sedan hissing with palsy on its way
to any given appliance store. She needed to return a defective toaster and hoped she
might run in to three young women plodding in the midst of damnation.

Thoughts on quasiloss...
Eli Galvan

Hard to really say in type what my fingers want to dance to. Numb fingers on black plastic alpha-numeric keys. The chase is over as early as it has begun. Can't chase a dream in true visceral reality. There are true unbreakable boundries; circumstance, feelings, professions, and ultimately the ocean. You can try the best you can. Sometimes it's good enough. For the most part it's all in vain. Statistically and on a big enough timeline, nothing lasts. We all hold onto the bits and fragments of joy hoping in our pathetic minds that it will LAST. I remember thinking when I was much younger that I wish I could hold onto my toys and having that initial joy forever. The gutteral truth that hit me then was that toys grow old just as we do. They break. The plastic luster faded, and the joints in GI Joe's legs broke. What is left to hold onto? I got a little sad. Hell, I got sad when my cheeseburger fell apart then. Shit happened. I dealt with it then. Maybe I cried a little. We all try so hard to immortalize the joy in any desperate way possible; a picture, a painting, writing, a voice message, a soon to fade memory... trying to re-live the past in a pathetic and obscure nostalgic fumbling... planting a seed and watching the flower die. Attempts at the multiple poly-hexagonal magnum opus in any way shape or form. Doing the dance to attract your mate. The one with the less attractive dance is alone and doesn't pass on his seed. My whole fist shaking has occurred at the peak of realization; there are no guarantees in anything. The sad thing is you can really only rely on yourself. Sad isn't it? It's why I am the way I am. Selfish as it sounds, it's safe for ME in the confines of my own insanity. I come out of the shell only when I feel the time is right just like a fucking turtle. I love who I have become. Nothing else really matters, and then something catches my attention... Something shiny, something beautiful... something so spectacularly reminiscent of my own self-discovery that I want to dance. Chills... the chills of grasping something so real. Once I've realized it was there, it disappeared; like a truth you can only whisper to one person at a time before it dissipates. My eyes blink like lenses on an excited camera. Last night felt like my eyes had chewed bubble gum. Cried through smoky contact lenses. Monosyllabic sighs... 3 of them before I slipped away tonight with the flavorless gum. Windows to the soul clouded with the morning mist upon my awakening.

Mono syllabic sighs... 3 of them. There they are again... this time without an utterance

Reflections On Finis
Alana Boldt

I remember August of 2003 vividly. It wasn't that anything spectacular happened that year, but it was the first time I heard of the 203-QQ47 asteroid. My wife of forty years, Sheila, and I first saw the news spot on CNN. We switched the television channels in hopes of getting more information on this curious phenomena. Just about all of the channels definitely downplayed any significance to the reports. One station stated there was only a 1 in 909,000 chance that an object from 'out there' just might come close to earth on March 21, 2014.

Within days of the initial reports, the story just dropped out of the media reports. No one was reporting on the event. It was as though the initial report had fallen into an abyss. Sheila thought she'd like to research the subject further. Perhaps it was her background, being of Hopi Indian decent, that she believed the ancient prophecies of her people were going to be fulfilled. The earth, according to Sheila, was headed for destruction. With great dedication, she began to research the prophecies of other ancient cultures.

The Mayan calendar alluded to a catastrophe of great magnitude; the calendar simply ended in the year 2012. Hieroglyphics discovered in the chamber of an Egyptian pyramid told of the time when a man would be born, and that he would be a king and leader of a great religious movement. These writing also end abruptly after indicating a mass destruction of the earth occurring approximately 2,000 years after the life of this man. Upon examination, even the Chinese I-Ching suggests the demise of this planet is inevitable in about the same time period.

I studied asteroids a bit, making notes in my journal. Together Sheila and I learned they are chunks of rock left over from the formation of our solar system 4.5 billion years ago. QQ47 just happened to be 1.2 kilometers wide and weighed about 2.6 billion tons. Astronomers were first able to view old 47 in October of 2003, but information was sparse. As the asteroid became slightly visible to the rest of us, it appeared to resemble a small blue star far in the distant night sky.

Still, the occurrence remained elusive from the ears of the population for the next several years. There simply were no further news reports or information given on 47. If the scientific community was learning and observing, they weren't sharing. Instead, news channels gave their attention to political scandals, wars, and the escapades of sports and movie celebrities. We were being entertained. We were not being informed. Most people simply forgot about any threat that might surface from space. Instead, the focus was on global warming and the obvious effects that it was causing.

It was the Fall of 2009 when QQ47 again was brought to the attention of earth's general population. There was no explanation as to why it had been put on some dusty shelf away from the eyes of humanity. Yes, QQ47 was alive and it appeared it was coming our way. The possibility this asteroid may collide with our planet was not a possibility, but rather a probability. The odds that it would collide with earth were 1 in 300. If QQ47 was going to impact earth, it would have the same effect as 20 million Hiroshima atomic bombs. Only the date of impact had been changed since the initial report of 2003. The suggested date of possible impact was given as November of 2011, a lot sooner than the original date the media had suggested!

It was about that time dramatic world-wide weather and nature changes began to occur. There were earthquakes, floods, droughts, tsunamis and storms of great magnitudes. We could only speculate if the conditions were due to global warming or perhaps something more sudden and intense. It was also about the time I started to journal.

Over the next months, we watched with awe in our planet's weather changes as it caused catastrophes beyond our realm of thought. I occasionally wrote in my journal as life around us changed. Humanity became increasingly aware of earth's future. Or I guess it might have been the lack of future that seemed to distress people. Religious communities grew as folks gravitated to the belief of their choice. A lot of folks were bound gain salvation, through God, Jesus, Allah, through the meditations of Buddhism, or to whoever else might listen.

Perhaps it was the hopes of salvation that guided a lot of people to become friendly, even helpful and actually attempted to gain a greater understanding of their neighbors. Food and clothing were sent to starving children and cultures across the continents. The population in nursing homes and homeless shelters dwindled as families and strangers opened their homes and hearts to take people in. People even finally accepted the most severely handicapped population, welcoming them into their churches and neighborhood groups. Most people became very friendly and really, really nice to each other. I think there were a lot of people who thought their eleventh hour acts of kindness just might buy their way into some utopian afterlife. Mankind hadn't gotten it right in so many millions of years; it now appeared they wanted to take a crash course in ethics and brotherly love.

Of course, there was the other side of good vs. evil, too. Suicides and suicide/murders did rise in numbers, about as dramatically as one might think. Crime and looting were also prevalent as the months just sort of flew by. There are always those people who think they might stockpile their material goods and take everything along, just in case they might be going somewhere. I remember joking with my friend Bob, a funeral home director, who said he couldn't recall even one instance of a U-Haul trailer backing up to his back door so folks could take things with them.

Liquor sales went up like a skyrocket, as did the use of drugs. Physicians were, and still are, passing out antidepressant and sedative prescriptions like candy. I can tell you the pharmaceutical companies have made a bundle of money on this! I have to chuckle when thinking what all of these people are going to do with their profits if old 47 does decide to make a direct hit. I guess this nation will play out Capitalism to what may, or may not, be the bitter end.

The differences in cultures and races that had been so prevalent in the past seemed to lose their importance. For the most part, people seemed to divide into categories. There are the calm and gentle ones who appeared to be making the proverbial lemons into lemonade. Then there are the mean-spirited ones who have climbed to the epitome of nasty. So many other folks simply reside in a perpetual state of hysteria. And there are those people who are still trying to bargain their way out of this grand event.

Groups of people have moved to the mountains, to the deserts, even underground. I have to smile at that one, too! Just where do people think they can hide? The circumstances of the past months have certainly brought out the best, and the worst, of mankind. The human spirit, it seems, is drawing strength in some sort of 'inner knowing'. But I can tell you that everyone, and I mean everyone, seems real, real nervous. Wasn't it Franklin D. Roosevelt who said, "There is nothing to fear...but fear itself."? I can't for the life of me understand the fear. Fear is the powerful, destructive emotion than can only survive in the future tense. Perhaps if some of these people would take solace in their past accomplishments, the time would be less chaotic. Or maybe some don't feel they've accomplished anything. It seems to me the thought of any man or woman not accomplishing anything good or decent in life is more frightening than any large rock coming from out of the sky!

Over the years my journal entries have been sporadic. I haven't exactly been faithful to my journal. But tonight, I find solace in the entries I did take time to write. My beloved Sheila died unexpectedly from a short-term cancer April 14th of 2010. She felt no pain. There was no suffering and I was happy for that. Although she was comfortable with what life, and death, had to offer, I knew she was upset with the possible demise of our planet. Paranoia had invaded our psyches. She ached not for herself, but for humanity as a whole, especially the children. She grieved deeply for the earth itself.

Our only son, Matt, succumbed to pneumonia just two months later, in June of 2010. He was 22 years old. He was the gentlest son a man could hope for and we were so very proud of him. Despite his cerebral palsy and mental retardation, he was a kind person, accepting whatever life, or people, had to offer him.

My dog Max died just three months ago. He crossed over as I held him on my lap right here in this recliner. He had been my best friend and companion since his birth seventeen years prior to his death. When it comes to the destruction of this world, I have no one to worry about, no one to grieve for if this is truly going to be 'the end'. I only feel sad knowing so many people, so many young souls, and aging entities may not be blessed with the full life Sheila, Matt, and I shared.

It is the eve of December 5th, 2011. Before the television stations stopped live reporting, they said scientists world-wide were doing all they knew how to do in their battle against destiny. The laser technology that sounded good in theory as a combatant to 47 did not prove to have enough destructive power against the asteroid. Earlier reports said the United States had made six attempts to divert the asteroid with nuclear warheads. India and Pakistan joined forces to release five warheads. Russia combined forces with China to launch eight attempts to project warheads around the perimeter of the asteroid in attempts to divert its path. Of course the politicians were right up front, still campaigning, when the newscasters filmed the frenzy at military bases around the world. I chuckle when thinking that just in case we come out of this alive, it'd be a good campaign platform.

There is an underlying feeling that we, the world, stand waiting on a hangman's platform. The noose is tight and we wonder if the lever will be released. I am sure many wonder what we did to 'deserve' this predicament. Perhaps it is what we didn't do. Now I have to wonder if old 47 doesn't knock us out of the game, would we still face the ancient prophecies of the winter solstice of 2012?

Live broadcasts on the television ceased. Stations are focused on airing religious themes. The churches, temples, mosques, and synagogues are packed full. But then so are the bars and city streets. Chaos is in abundance. There are so many souls in obvious fear and distress. The masses are praying for retrieval, a miracle. Some wave banners of hope, while others gallantly prepare for an Armageddon. Some people cry out in madness, while others don't appear to be effected, as though it is 'time'. I suppose each soul must listen to its own inner voice, its own heartbeat.

My neighbor Joe stopped by earlier. He wanted to know if I'd like to join his family for dinner and then go to a church. He's been a good friend, but I'd sort of like to be alone. I feel fine right here at home. It is quiet and it is comfortable. I feel the presence of my Sheila, Matt and old Max. It is time to rest now and lay aside this worn journal. I do wonder if I have made my last entry, or if perhaps there will be another, new paragraph to add some morning in the future.

Whatever happens, I know it really doesn't matter. Whatever QQ47 decides to do, it will be alright.

The Truth Behind Myself
Jennifer Kelmer

Consumed with your own surroundings you forget about what you see
All she wants is approval
All she wants is to be the same
All she wants is to be happy for once
She cannot hide her pain
It bursts from every inch of her body
It screams
All she wants is to be free
Free from all the rules of Normality
Free from her self
She is so sad inside and out
You forget to look past her body
Look into her soul
This is where it LIES
Her inner secrets her hidden identity
Day after day she begins to fall
Deeper and deeper into false reality
Demons and Gods appear all around
Her sadness is gone but she isn't who she says she is
False Reality

The Branding of Herald
Part 1
Wes Rader

He reached out of his bed and pointed at Phil, the fat goldfish that Jed had won at the fair right before Cheryl realized how much of a screw up Herald had become. Herald needed a stiff drink. He slowly rolled out of his bed, letting the blankets fall to the floor. Lovingly he fed Phil and walked out of their bedroom. Sliding his worn Pumas over his toes to his ankles while walking toward the door in the same pair of gym shorts and Guinness T-shirt he had worn yesterday and quite possibly the day before that. Herald left the small apartment and began walking toward the liquor store. It was early in the morning at least for him but he knew Curvies opened at 11am so he had no quarrels with getting up so early to squall some booze. It had been uncommonly hot this summer for Minnesota, as beads of sweat dripped down his balding head, making his glasses slide agitatedly down his nose. The sidewalk was chipped and the grass was dying but the flowers that the old man in 104 had planted in early spring were taking well to the daily care. That's all that old man ever did. On the corner of his street he glared at his beaten down Ford pickup that gave up on him two weeks ago from tomorrow.

The rattled old Ford had been acting up or awhile now and now the mechanic wants 800$ just to put a new transmission in not to mention the 75 that he hadn't paid him to tow it to that corner so it could torment him every time he walked by. He had bought the truck from his cousin and still owed him a few weeks work for it. Herald's cousin Mike had a lawn care service that was just starting up. Mike decided when he lost his live-in girlfriend to his unhealthy habits of dope and videogames that he needed to get a real job. Mike had started with his old pickup truck and one push mower. Three years later he had bought a used truck, trailer and three riding mowers. Herald always liked working lawn care because he could sip all day long to make his buzz that much smoother to the transition to evening of beers and liquor shots. On the days he would actually go to work he would always be the first one on site so he could have the tractor with the best cup holder. Though his cousin told him that he would rather him drink soda or water for legal reasons. Herald reasoned with the idea and for the respect of his cousin he started to put his sauce in an apple juice bottle to keep suspicions down. God, this was a longer walk than he remembered. Herald looked at his plump belly as he pulled uncomfortably against his t shirt. He looked into the reflection from a parked minivan window. She probably left because of this as he looked in self somber. That's why; how could she be so shallow? He pondered if he would have done the same.

Gemini Child
Amber McClellan

Sugarbaby was a being from the sea
soggy then covered with shells and sand
her voice was raw and gentle
but only to those as natural as she

Dot was more mature and held a key
to questions of youth in her faux pearl strand
and floppy straw hat, though often temperamental
confidence and loyalty were her guarantee

They've gone and left a conscientious decree
A cold, destructive actuality close at hand
creases the forehead, purpose is a material
artful chore—sorting through debris

Concentration
Amber McClellan

Honeybee lands on my hand
at the beach
an attempted personal day
overripe mango for lunch
reason is carried away
the bee must've drunk through
the sweet
how delightful
to so easily disregard the sour

47

Fisherman on El Prado
Amber McClellan

His suitcase did not hold relics of a past life—
no pictures, newspaper clippings, children's chipped
paintings withered with age.
It did not contain a suit and tie, a comb or shampoo.
While walking concentric cubes, galoshes squeaking,
he did not mumble incoherent thoughts or profanities
or idly wait for change.
His fishing hat was worn not dirty.

8:30am approaching with care
I offered a steaming cup of coffee.
His face was tanned, unshaven
his silver whiskers trembled when he replied
"Thank-you," without looking up he turned
and began to walk out his measured course.

"What's in the case?" I asked, hoping to engage
but sounding forceful and sarcastic.

When he turned, he lifted his head
his eyes were not dull or resentful.

He straightened his hunch,
hoisted the suitcase onto a table.
Unlocking both clasps,
He flipped a switch
Leadbelly drowned the dreary morning with

"Where did you sleep last night?"
from a squawking 45.

Gray's Ending
Eric Petty

Known throughout my family as the dreaded affliction, the plague of today's children, a sickness infecting only spoiled, rebellious children who never minded their parents, uncertainty, my father told me, was my worst enemy. My father also warned me that an idle mind was the devil's workshop. None of which I believed as true. Yet, my idle mind would be educated, stifling the idleness, which is child.

Admittedly, I wandered a little too far, day dreamed a little too long, but there was never uncertainty in my actions just an insatiable curiosity and an occasional lapse in judgement. Without this dreaded affliction, the incredible story I am about to tell you may never have occurred.

On an early November evening of my junior year at Cambridge, I walked upon fallen, autumn leaves blowing from the woods surrounding the university covering the paths to the library; my weekly haunt. I was thinking quietly to myself, entranced in the past by the thought of a girl named Jacqueline I acquainted at the beginning of my freshmen year. She had a beauty that I had never encountered before, although I am not sure quite what it was about her. Whether 'twas the way her auburn hair fell upon her eyes so blue like the reflection of September sky on a flowing stream or her pearlish smile, coy in its genesis and mysterious as it faded. There was not a single part of her I did not know and did not memorize. The small of her back, the stride of her step, even the deepness of her breath certainly avoiding the dying gasps of Caesar. All of her completed inside my heart, stored and tapped.

I had the unnatural notion that I would marry her. Call it intuition. Call it karma. Call it foolish.

She had not met many friends in the limited time she attended Cambridge. She was alone and she decided to attend another university in the south where a young man named Jameson Monroe coincidentally enrolled that fall semester. From what I understood, Jameson courted her in such an austere way I could have kicked myself when I heard of his method: He asked her to dance at a university social function; the genius in simplicity. She was so overwhelmed by his outward friendliness that she immediately fell for him.

I could certainly have approached her in such a fashion surpassing the charismatic, albeit simple way of one Jameson Monroe. Yet, I never had the opportunity to approach her as I spied her only from a far, chivalrous distance. Too uncertain was I to make acquaintances with such a flaxen, alpine lady. Uncertainty abolished my chance with the girl I loved and never knew; hence the name dreaded affliction.

49

Alas, the memory was still haunting me this chilled, November evening, but the face I captured in my thoughts warmed me on those long walks trudging through the mass of dried, summer leaves. One certain, although unwarranted, idea I often ruminated was that we were a match made in heaven.

Inside the library, I found my favorites resting silently, huddled together in the long wooden shelves. Dickens, Poe, Wells, Whitman, Tennyson and other leather bound novels of time, despair, love and hope. On this night, greeting the works I so admired, I happened upon a queer colored leather copy. Obviously misplaced next to Lord Tennyson sat a diary. A strange, discolored book aged years before its time by dust and misuse. I was intrigued by its demise.

Inside inscribed by the shaky hand of a would-be lunatic read the story of Sir Francis Lord Burroughs. Written ten years earlier, in 1897, it explained the phenomenal life of an inventor, alchemist, poet and hopeless romantic.

The diary began hazily on an evening much like the night I discovered the book. He wrote of his undying love for his dear Lydia and the choice he made to leave her at her darkest hour. All Lord Burroughs' passages were written in a special room or 'chamber' as he called it. His writing struggled to bring to life the emotions he felt, but as I believed no words could convey the feelings he felt for his dear Lydia. Interrupting the prosetic passages were several poems for his Lydia. Watching her in his memory walking through the field of gerbera daisies drifting paisley, summer dress in her contented wake among the faeries caring for the blooming, cotton blossoms.

As I flipped through the quill written pages, several newspaper clippings dropped to the floor. One such clipping examined the mysterious fire at the old O'Connor mansion many years ago. The fire had burned over three-quarters of the mansion taking the life of Mrs. Jonathan O'Connor and her unborn child. The fire was chronicled by would be journalist and Cambridge theologian, Professor Emmanuel Favret.

Favret's discourse speculatively examined weather patterns, eyewitnesses and police documentation of the fire. One witness reported having seen a greenish lightning bolt discharge from an absolutely clear sky into the mansion setting the roof ablaze.

Yet another witness's testimonial swore upon St. Peter that he had seen a greenish porthole envelope the sun drenched, cloudless sky then release a strange light that bounced upon the mansion's slate roof settling close to the chimney spreading across the roof subsequently causing the blaze.

Police reports ascertained the chimney spat out an ember that caused the deadly blaze.

Jacqueline O'Connor and child were pronounced dead at 3:11 p.m., August 31, two days after the fire. A heartfelt obituary written by Lord Burroughs accompanied the article. That incidental Tuesday was the first day of my freshman year. It was also the day I first set eyes on Jacqueline. A day I will never forget.

Another article profiled Lord Burroughs as a philanthropic eccentric living in a modest home outside Cambridge. It also told of the incredible inventions and ideas that he brought to the people of the village. Many were so ingenious; the scientific community referred to him as, "the Lord with the mind of a god."

As there were articles extolling his remarkable genius, testimonials written by much the same journalists and Sir Francis Lord Burroughs himself examined the ludicrous journey he had taken to become the man he was, where he was. These articles were published days proceeding the commendatory features. Madman and lunatic were but the kindest of words characterizing Lord Burroughs, he himself weaving a tapestry of negativity directed wholly at himself immortalized in the annals of the Cambridge Press.

Each day, a single solitary page from within the beaten diary recorded a gradual mental and physical decline of Lord Burroughs. Then there were but blank pages in this biography of the fallen demigod.

Armed with my affliction, I searched for hours trying to find an accompaniment to the volume of the fantastic journey I had just witnessed in paper.

After my profitless search, I decided to roam through the lengthy library of past Cambridge Press newspapers in hopes of finding the conclusion to this story I so feverishly enjoyed.

Suddenly, my thoughts usually reserved completely for my own lost love were overpowered with the mystery of Sir Francis Lord Burroughs. It was not an absolutely welcome exchange; more a brief respite from what I was sure would be an eternity before, if ever, I forgot her face.

Hidden deep within the ever dry walls of the Cambridge Press basement were an assortment of articles either directly or indirectly naming Lord Burroughs to some high honor bestowed to him by the eternally, if not fickle, Cambridgeians or a group of patrons involved in an operation sponsored by Burroughs. In either instance, Burroughs was well appreciated and honored so.   Of the dozen or so articles concerning Lord Burroughs, it seems as if the few negative articles outweighed the dozens of positive. It seems that Burroughs may have masterminded the negative publicity himself in order to escape into the world where his dear Lydia quietly awaited his sleep; a little slice of death.

Though the articles either hailed or condemned Lord Burroughs, one vital piece was missing: the obituary. As I searched it, became apparent that the man was still very much alive, yet secluded somewhere in the surrounding hillside.

On Wednesday, after a two-hour lecture from professor Favret, a stout man with perpetually windblown, greying hair inevitably sticking to his spectacles, on the role of Theology in society, I noticed an unfamiliar man talking to the professor. He was tall and slender with willowy fingers writing feverishly with a new type of pencil, working with the capacity of a quill encased in a shiny cover and a seemingly endless supply of ink without a well. This new device was termed a roller-ball-tip marking pen. Strange.

I am not for certain, but I think I tied my shoe sixteen times while I listened to the purposely-hushed conversation before me. He had introduced himself to my professor as Marcus DePasqualle, a close, personal friend of Lord Burroughs. Professor Favret admitted he hadn't heard that name for many years and asked of the Lord's health and residence. Marcus, disappointedly, declined to answer as to the wishes of his confidant.

I was unable to comprehend many questions due to their complexity, fortunately, my shoe would not stay tied so I was able to fake my preoccupation long enough to find a clue.

DePasqualle dropped a card on the floor as he removed it from his breast pocket. On this hardened piece of thick paper was an address. Whose address I was not sure, but it was the fertile ground from which my investigation blossomed.

The address belonged to Marcus DePasqualle. He lived in a small, stone masoned home several miles outside Cambridge, about an hour ride on my bicycle.

Outside, the home looked as if deserted by many years, but as I knocked and DePasqualle answered I felt I was standing at the gates of heaven. The paradise before me smelled of fresh air and life. Abundant, green foliage encompassed every inch of the interior while vibrant chamber music echoed through the spacious halls.

I must have been in awe a might too long for DePasqualle actually shook my shoulder to bring me out of my induced state. He greeted me and I introduced myself as a student of history. I told him I was interested in the amazing life of Lord Burroughs. He watched me closely as he asked me in his wispy French accent how I came to such knowledge of his acquaintance to Lord Burroughs. I lied and told him I figured it out from a photograph imposed on an article of Lord Burroughs and himself being awarded an honorarium. It was all a lucky guess, I told him, not to mention a particularly stubborn shoelace. He smiled and invited me into his establishment.

As I scanned my surroundings I gathered he was an avid admirer of classical music and antiques. Many vases and colored glasses broke the monopoly of greenery while chestnut and mahogany furniture sat patiently in a preordained arrangement. One solitary violin weeped gracefully in a distant room.

DePasqualle wandered off into the pantry and returned with a try of steaming, Earl Grey tea. He, not surprisingly, had many questions for his intrusive visitor. My full name, residence, college standing, reason for this inquisition and others asked quickly as to confuse a deceitful mind. Uncertainty, proved very useful for I had little knowledge of most the topics he had questioned me.

I had only a few concrete questions to use to pull the confidential information from him. When I asked between sips of too hot tea, he merely declined to answer staring off into some distant area or walking to his plants giving them an impromptu pruning. Silence was the ultimate foil.

In my expressionless exasperation, I began to examine the many pictures covering the manicured, defoliated walls. Within each framed, colorless photo lived his many friends and acquaintances, most abundantly was the gently smiling Lord Burroughs. DePasqualle expounded, in detail, on every nook and cranny of each picture. He explained that it was Lord Burroughs who had first introduced him to the science of botany and his subsequent love of flora.

In one particular photo, Lord Burroughs and DePasqualle stood outside a home laughing at some indefinable remark. As Marcus viewed the photo, he smiled like a child watching the rainfall through a timeless, summer day.

Behind them, an unfamiliar dwelling stood with the house numbers entirely visible. To the left of the building a blurred, partially perceptible street sign sprouted, stifled by the stop motion of the photograph. 423 Manche...

I assumed this to be the residence of Lord Burroughs and quickly developed an excuse to retire from Marcus DePasqualle's residence. He understood and thanked me for the company. Needless to say, I felt as if I had betrayed him serving only to quench my uncertain curiosity. Yet, somewhere in the oak bathed countryside lived the purpose of my deceitful act.

For two days the cold, November rain kept me from venturing to the assumed residence of Lord Burroughs, but my thoughts were wholly concerned with his life.

A break in the dreary weather gave me ample opportunity to search for the infamous house. I started off early as the sun and expectations woke me on that incidental Saturday. My mind wandered into areas unforgiving when brought into reality. Yet, when an answer to an intriguing question awaits in some exotic far away land, one can only dream.

I had envisioned Lord Burroughs working in a garden perhaps dreaming up some incredible device to aid all mankind or maybe he had found a suitable mate that healed the heart that seemed so hopelessly broken. Many ideas of the expected discovery fumbled through my mind. Some were simple like a man just living in a house outside Cambridge, while others were extraordinarily complex starting with him being the incarnation of a sentient being sent down to Earth healing the ails of man and society ending with Lord Burroughs returning to society after a thirty year sabbatical saving the human race from their sinful demise. In all, I had envisioned him being the man he once was, happy and content in a life he once occupied so astonishingly.

Manchester Lane was a small, cobblestone drive leading into a well-to-do community south of the university. I can still, to this day, remember the teeth chattering I received as I turned onto the cobblestone inlaid road.

Brick and stone houses lined each side of the road running east/west. I could see shimmering, metal appliances occupying countertops as woven tapestries diffused the peering eyes of curious onlookers. The look and feel of wealth saturated the vista as I clamored along the tightly, packed cobbles.

Among the inordinate display of wealth was one loathsome dwelling suffering from years of inattention. As I neared the frightful house, the numbers 423 became visible. My thoughts and dreams were almost vanquished, yet a reprieve still flickered in the back of my mind. Marcus DePasqualle's home was as ragged, well not quite, as the presupposed home of Lord Burroughs. Perhaps the disdained fascad portrayed by DePasqualle's home would be the mask of Lord Burroughs' as well.

As I neared the masoned continental, I spied many the same floras as in DePasqualle's home. A quilt of wild fern grew rampant slowly invading a path of ivory lilacs ever fighting the tightening grip of winter. Amber blades of grass grappled with licentious sage in a sobering mosaic sprawling the lawn. Diseased rose bushes unsuccessfully battled hungry wrens devouring the delicious petals from the flowers' thorny grasp.

Evergreen bushes cascaded onto the entrance leading up to the front door. Rainwater dripping from a decaying hole in the slate roof crept unabated into the quadruple, stone supports rising from the achy, wooden floorboards.

Hesitantly, I addressed the wooden door with my fisted knuckles, softly at first as to not attract attention.
Realizing my idiocy, I followed with powerful sequence of pounding. An eerie silence followed. I turned to leave carefully watching my step avoiding the rotting, porch boards when a slow, numbing crawl of the door from its jamb crept up my spine. I had begun to wonder if this investigation had any further purpose or meaning. Anything would surely have been more suiting than witnessing the loathsome sight I beheld.

Before me sat Sir Francis Lord Burroughs.

The man who had brought inventions, speculations and animation to this small community sat disquieted in a rickety, wooden wheelchair. The damp smell of sickness rushed through my senses as it scampered out the open door to mix with the fresh, November air.

"Please, come in." he said as he turned and rolled into the middle of the purple and grey wallpapered atrium. The stifled, ambient light falling in from a space in a wooden board covering one window gave a haunted, uneasy character to the living room. I walked carefully behind Lord Burroughs as he pulled me further into his private, haunted sanctuary.

A slight breeze drifted past an open hallway. I closed my eyes tightly afraid to witness the ghostly tenant slowly dying in the eternal winds. Oak floorboards moaned a sorrowful sigh under the weight of its two wanderers.

"Mr. DePasqualle said I might be receiving a visitor soon." he remarked to the hallway in which we traveled. "I rather enjoy the company. I find it very stimulating to talk to young minds. Especially those attend such a prestigious university." He mentioned as his head gently turned to my attention.

"How do you know where I attend college?" I asked, intrigued at this man's apparent knowledge of a person to whom he'd never been introduced.

"DePasqualle told me of your fascination with a specific photograph at his residence. It was a photo of him and me standing in front of this very house. The address wasn't completely visible, but discernable to able minded, college educated man such as you. That is how you came to be in my home, is it not?"

I thought for a minute pondering the question. While I had no other options, lies and deceptions rolled through my mind trying to pull together a viable excuse for my uninvited intrusion into this man's ostensibly, diseased world.

"Yes it is Lord Burroughs. I was interested in the interesting life you've chosen to ignore." Perhaps I had overstepped my bounds in saying so, but it gave him the definite reason for my being there. I prepared for a scolding remark, but he simply continued to wheel himself through the narrow hall as if I wasn't an accompaniment.

"You are familiar with my life, are you?" he asked bemused at the sudden attention he'd received from my candid remark.

"I've taken an interest in your life story through the readings I have found in your diary I accidentally came across at the university library." For some reason I figured him as being hard of hearing and talked loudly, enunciating my every syllable.

"You read somewhere in my diary I had lost my hearing, did you?", Lord Burroughs countered. A hint of humor tinted his words. I did not reply for we both knew the answer; my imagination getting ahead of me. Mind you, it was very easy concerning the environment I had encountered in his home.

I saw a soft light growing away from a space between the raw, wooden floorboards and the flaking skin of the tattered hallway door. My heart beat rampantly as I expected the soul center of this house to bear the true brunt of the disease.

Behind the door, opened forcibly by the footholds of the wooden wheelchair, glowed a fantastically, white chamber.

Light drenched every aspect of this room like the accusing, examination light of a medical practitioner. Windowless walls erected from the white, tiled floor defiantly protected Lord Burroughs. A solitary, oaken desk, in its polished luster, crouched in the apex of two combating walls. Upon this desk, a maroon, leather copy sat open with one of the new types of pencils Marcus DePasqualle had occupying the gut disrupted in mid-thought by my infringement. A fine China plate balanced precariously against the wall.

I squinted momentarily adjusting to the overpowering white. The sterility of the room so surprised me I could hardly manage to retain my gasp. This was his chamber. The quiet room he wrote the original, aged volume of his life littered with poems for his dear Lydia. This room was the embodiment of his mind.

He wheeled in before me settling before the desk, his hand resting gently upon his thoughts written in the diary. I followed in behind, sitting lightly upon a flowery, fustian loveseat.

"You say you are interested in my life, the one I have chose to ignore, is that correct?" He leaned back confidently in his wheelchair. My eyes a cluster with the unexpected surroundings affixed on Lord Burroughs, the first exposed sight I had of him.

I drew a deep, frightened breath as I beheld him sitting there so casually, confidently covered with patches of white cotton matted onto his face, his mouth nearly covered by the encroaching white. Once blue denim faded carelessly at his knees while thick, woolen socks lazily covered his feet. A discolored toenail poked through a worn stitch in the stocking.

A thick, black beard hung inconspicuously below the mass of cotton nearly touching the fleece, senescent sweater as a whisper of odor lingered towards me.

"You are very quiet for such an inquisitive man. Another man might be judgmental under such circumstances, but you....you take a quiet solace in this admittedly chaotic home. That is admirable, is it not?" As he spoke he rapped his fingers in sequence upon the desk. Each nail delicately manicured to a lovely arch stretching from the pinkest of fingers. I wondered why the rest of his body, not to mention his home, was in such entropy while his hands were lovely and welcoming. Perhaps spending so much time pulled tight into the well of the desk disallowed him to view his lower half and his face would be only visible in the instance he had a mirror. But these chamber walls were only covered with calendars. Every month of the year was clearly visible from his desk. In crimson ink, the words 'Lydia at 3:10' occupied the Tuesdays on every calendar. I suppose the calendars and his hands were his immediately visible items in this domain. It was specific by design.

A darkened afterimage of a crucifix loomed heavily over his desk.

"I didn't mean any disrespect by my remark; I just thought you should fully understand the intentions behind my visit." I found it difficult to tend this bizarre man as my eyes anxiously wondered the room searching for an article to which I could distractedly affix. Yet, as I sat there I became strangely interested in his disheveled attire. While his appearance was odd and somewhat frightening, the gentle beauty in his hazel green eyes peering from beneath the ragged cut of his hair quieted my unease. I settled back into the small sofa letting the flowery pattern absorb me.

"Lord Burroughs, I am delighted that you have allowed me to enter your home without appointment. My name is..." and I reached out my hand to shake. His eyes glared silently at the extended mass of flesh. He never grasped its welcome.

"I know who you are son. Mr. DePasqualle has spoken of you. I must say I am quite flattered at your preoccupation with my life. Most people have either forgotten or dismissed my existence. I can't imagine why..." as he spoke, a piece of pillowy cotton fell from his face landing on the floor inches from the wheelchair footholds. Gracefully he bent over to replace the wandering piece of cotton. His prematurely aged bones creaked and

56

cracked under the unexpected bending as he delicately placed the cotton back to its rightful position on his soiled, unshaven face. Undaunted by the unusualness of the act, he continued with his observation, "why a person would bother with an ordinary man like myself. I am glad to see the youth of this community caring so much about its elders that is indeed enough appointment for me to talk with you. Now what is it you wish to talk about?"

"First of all, Lord Burroughs, you had the social class, scientific community and the university astonished by your inventiveness, as soon as it all started, it was over. Why?"

"Actually, son, I found that most of those groups you mentioned actually wanted the commercial success I could offer. So their portrayal as loyal citizens to my practice is unfounded. After the deluge of my inventions began to trickle, the scientific community was first to castrate my scientific practice. The university moving quickly behind aptly suspended my stipend. And as you know the social class is linked heavily with the university consisting largely of boosters and alumni. So you see, son, I was a pawn in their political chess match. Besides, I believe it was time for me to retire." He seemed convinced of his manufactured rejection. On his desk he rapped his fingernails lightly.

"Looking through the articles in your diary I found at the library and articles in the Cambridge Press, I'd say you did it yourself making a mockery of your own achievement. I read several articles that you penned denouncing everything you ever accomplished. One of your articles even mentioned that you shouldn't even be here. But because of some incredibly mysterious experiment that you concocted, you are stuck here in another place and time. What does that mean? Why would someone who has all this to share with the world simply give up and become a recluse?" My heart beat rampantly. I had just called this man a liar to his face, in his own house, for no reason other than my own pretentious curiosity.

"In what article did you read about the experiment? Are you sure you didn't get that information from that moronic theologian, Professor Favret?", he candidly asked.

"In a round about way, yes. It was an article in one of the papers I found in the basement of the Press." I paused watching Lord Burroughs sigh heavily, "I think Professor Favret is on your side anyway. He asked Mr. DePasqualle of your health just last week." Burroughs looked perplexed by my insight. Perhaps I shouldn't have mentioned I had knowledge of the meeting between DePasqualle and Favret. If Burroughs was trying to seclude himself in the countryside never to be bothered or heard from again, my covertly gained knowledge could mean others had the opportunity to hear that private conversation.

"You know of that meeting, do you?" he examined.

"Class was in session that day DePasqualle joined Professor Favret. I was in the front row. Since I was already at a dead-end with no other influences other than the diary and a few press clippings, I had to eavesdrop slightly." I nervously bit my lip as I ended my confession.

"I'd say your eavesdropping served its purpose. What else do you know about that meeting? Did you hear everything they talked about? Did you notice his new writing utensil?" He leaned forward peering at me through the mass of cotton with his hazel eyes.

"I heard everything they said, but I couldn't comprehend the majority of it. It's only my first semester of Theology." feeling his persistent stare, I stood and wandered anxiously about the room with my hands tucked tightly in my front pockets, "Professor Favret was thrown by some of the questions. I don't think he had the answers DePasqualle was searching for and his new writing utensil was very nice, I suppose"

"With all his righteous indignation, Favret is not as intelligent as he thinks he is. He's a genius at speculation and assumption. Theological metaphysics is not his strongest area of concentration." He turned to his desk and opened the leather-bound diary to a dog-eared page and began reading to himself refreshing his memory. I wandered past his desk and from over his shoulder I noticed a detailed drawing of some machine with notes and arrows pointing to various mechanical positions occupying one of the pages.

"Theological metaphysics?" I asked. His attention returned to attend his uninvited company.

"A frequently overlooked branch of physics, but an incredibly important science nonetheless. It is the study of the grey area outside the reach of ordinary physics surpassing the theories brought forth by the father of metaphysics, Aristotle. But his theories are flawed for they were developed in a time of mythology, not Christianity. Our God has an incredible influence on time and space. You believe in God, do you not?" He questioned pointing an inquisitive finger at me motioning that I should return to the loveseat.

"Of course I believe in God." I answered slowly sitting down on the couch.

"Then you believe in the soul as the force behind our very existence?" Burroughs questioned.

"I know that's what separates us from the animals. An incomprehensible being of incredible power and understanding predestines the soul. He is what created everything in the universe." I stated glancing at the calendars. 'Lydia at 3:10' flashed before me eyes. Was he hallucinating her presence at 3:10 every Tuesday? In this spectrally sated dwelling I couldn't dismiss that as a possibility.

"You then believe in destiny and fate, do you not?" His wheelchair inched closer to me examining my forthcoming answer.

"I suppose so. I think destiny controls your life and fate controls your death. If anything, you could attempt to control destiny. You make the decisions that affect the important aspects of your own life, like learning to ride a bike or falling in love." I said matter of factly.

"Riding a bike, yes. You can even control the type of bike, the speed of which you ride, the areas you wish to ride through, everything. But love..." his eyes glazed over momentarily thinking in some different far-away place. A smile crept weakly from the corners of his lips, "Son, love is even more uncontrollable than death. Love is determined by every living being in the universe. The birds, the trees, the wandering fish swimming against seemingly insurmountable currents to fulfill his paternal duty. Love takes the energy from every possible living source and channels it into the bodies of man and woman. This energy is the most pure and powerful source of energy in the universe. It cannot be created or destroyed existing on heaven and Earth and in every plane of consciousness. Where death happens unexpectedly, inextricably, love cannot happen because it already is." He stopped and watched for my reaction.

"Like a match made in heaven." I added

"Yes, son, that is exactly what I mean." He settled back into his wheelchair content in my understanding. His eyes glossed over, thinking deeply. He had an almost hurt expression on his face. "You know, son, I haven't heard that expression in many years."

"You wrote it yourself in the diary I found at the library." I commented trying to refresh his memory.

"I must get that volume from the library before everyone knows my business." He ended and turned into the belly of the desk. Picking up his writing pencil-thing, he began jotting down an idea in his journal. His obtrusive, heavy handed clock dangled from his hand with the face telling the time. 3:05.

"Lord Burroughs? Have I said something to offend you? I didn't mean any.." and as I stood to address his desk, he pointed at me with the writing utensil.

"You should leave, son. I have some errands I have to attend to immediately." His writing utensil returned to his scribbling page in the diary.

I eased back in my stance and slowly walked towards the door. I felt disappointed not seizing an opportunity to ask him some important questions. Actually, I didn't really have any potentially revealing questions to ask. Truthfully, I went to Burroughs' home with no prearranged questions or topics.

I wasn't sure I would ever see Lord Burroughs again and that made it all the more difficult to accept the fact I would potentially never find out answers to certain perplexing questions. Was the cotton masking a horrible facial disfigurement? Why was 'Lydia at 3:10' on all the Tuesdays? What caused his catastrophic fall from grace?

As I opened the door to return into the disjointed reality outside Lord Burroughs' pristine chamber, I glanced back to catch a parting glimpse of this lonely man. There he sat, wheelchair pulled tight into the belly of the wooden desk scribbling frantically in his diary like a painter fighting unsuccessfully to capture a moment of a determined setting sun.

I muttered a brief farewell not expecting an answer. Closing the door behind me, I hurriedly walked down the yellowed hallway. The disease I once felt so overpowering somehow seemed dampened like sadness crying deeply never to be consoled.

As I entered into the atrium of the living room, my eyes adjusted to the lack of light. The wallpaper on the wall adjacent to the front door was peeled away to the bare plaster. On this wall, a contented woman walked through a field of cotton blossoms in bloom smiling at a timeless remark. Her eyes almost living in its immortal, blue stare following my every step. I stopped to admire the portrait growing from the ground to the crux of the wall and the ceiling fifteen feet above. Only one woman in Lord Burroughs' time, any time, could be so lovely. It was his dear Lydia.

I approached the massive mural to admire her painted beauty. Upon the painted field of cotton blossoms she danced were supplanted bits of white cotton rising slightly from the oiled veneer. Several puffs escaped from the lower brushed blossoms the oil smeared and chafed by movement of the unknowing painter. Translucent faeries laughed, bounding from flower to flower beneath Lydia's wind-blown dress, sunlight irradiating upon her waifish face. A puff of cotton stuck to her cheek, established in the dried oil feet from my attempted reach. I looked for a ladder or chair, but the atrium was barren holding no furniture and no matter how hard I tried to remove it, the height of her face was an insurmountable barrier.

As my vision tracked across the painted surface, I noticed scratched markings, almost smeared by someone's exasperated attempts at removal. So there it stayed, the cotton, unfortunately stuck to her timeless, painted face hidden by the unwelcome darkness in the atrium.

I took one last glance at the foreboding, chamber door. Hearing Lord Burroughs' wheelchair squeak slightly across the chamber floor, I privileged another glanced at Lydia and walked from his home. Lydia followed me out with a smile.

I had class the following day, Wednesday. Professor Favret talked endlessly, it seemed, yet I don't remember what exactly he spoke of for my mind was wandering Lord Burroughs' house following the lines of Lydia's face captured in a happier time when he knew her embrace. I could see how he became the man he is. From inventive genius to lonely recluse, she was there with him. Through the dramatic beginning to this humble repose, she gave her unyielding presence. The painting in his house was all he needed.

Gray's Quadrangle housed my dorm room. A beautiful granite, three-story structure with Gothic architecture characterized the exterior with a dark, stained mahogany finish inside. This particular dormitory was once the famous poet Thomas Gray's residence during his tenure at Cambridge. Gray was not fully appreciated or understood while at Cambridge. Matter of factly, he was despised by students and faculty alike.

His untimely death occurred after a practical joke played on him by his history students, who were disheartened by Gray for he was the only history professor who refused to lecture leaving entire books to be read without any insightful diction.

On a cold January eve in 1771, while Gray diligently composed a poem in Latin entitled, "Ode on the Death of a Favourite Cat, Drowned in a Tub of Gold Fishes", the student body carried a water barrel to a spot directly underneath his second story room. Engrossed in his writing, he panicked when he heard the cries of 'Fire' coming from outside. Gray without hesitation threw the Cambridge fire escape, consisting of five bedsheets tied together with knots every foot, out the window and scurried down the side of the granite building falling back first into the frigid water amidst the robust laughter of the Cambridge student body. Gray unfortunately caught pneumonia and died a week later.

The strange thing about this incident is it was not the first time that this prank had been pulled on Gray. Actually, it was seventh. The student body felt so badly about Gray's death, that they petitioned to have the Quadrangle memorialized and named in his honor. His colleagues were sent to immortalize his room by cleaning and organizing. They had discovered his affairs in order. Not the writings or teaching schedules, but wills and living testaments if anything unforeseen should happen to him. A few of his colleagues were convinced his accidental death was predetermined with evidence to support the claim such as his depression, seclusion and cryptic writing. His friends remained, although, convinced of his unfortunate and accidental death.

I lived in the room neighboring Gray's old room now considered a museum, cleaned frequently and often visited. On cold evenings, I swear I can hear the faint call of a quill pencil hurriedly marking a page in rhyme. Education, after all, does not completely cure the idle mind. Just keeps it occupied.

With my head hanging off the end of my bed, I watched an oak outside my window draw shapes with the moonlight. The ceiling was the canvas. I noticed an ink pencil, two types of flowers, a cobblestone road and Lydia all dancing in shadows on my ceiling. Strange how your mind decides what it wants to see. Sleep.

The next morning, I awoke with an excruciatingly stiff neck. I noticed a note had been slipped beneath my door. It clung strangely to the stained, oak trim lining the recently installed fireproof, asbestos tiles.

As I picked up the note, I glanced at the picture of my father I had tacked to my bulletin board earlier in the semester. It was of him standing in front of an Italian restaurant he built and operated with the help of my mother. He and my mother know everyone in the community that frequented their restaurant. Employees and customers alike refer to them as Mr. and Mrs. Rossini; a mistake easily made for Rossini's is the name of the restaurant, which they operate. To avoid embarrassment, everyone usually calls them Mr. and Mrs.

My father knows how to construct and fix anything with the most unusual devices, manufactured with his hands, developed from his mind. He was always trying to teach me how to fix a door or grease a wheel with the commonest of materials. Most were from our pantry at home. If he couldn't fix it with a bar of soap or a twist twine, then it was truly broken and unable to be fixed. On those occasions I would take it upon myself to fix those stubborn devices, succeeding on occasion. I learned a few tricks from my father. He would eventually notice it was fixed and assume it was he who tackled the enormous job of reglazing the window. My mother would kiss him on the cheek as reward and they would be none the wiser. I smile remembering. My eyes blink bringing me back to the note I held in my hand.

The note was from Lord Burroughs. Hand written in much the same style as his writings in the leather bound diary: hurried and abrupt. Upon this paper read, "Tuesday-1:00p.m.".

I arrived at Lord Burroughs' residence a half an hour early on Tuesday. DePasqualle was unexpectedly visiting, busily rebrushing a spot on Lydia's painted self, humming a quiet tune to the rhythm of his reconstructive brush.

Inside, I found the chaotic form of the home I once knew calm and ambivalent. Sunlight of the cloudless, November day drenched the atrium in a yellow cascade striking a bright arrangement of flowers in bloom occupying a far wall. The purplish tint of the wallpaper covering the atrium walls took on a lighter shade of blue. There were plants and abundant life inside this home and a statue of a handsome man standing next to the painting of Lydia. I hadn't noticed it on my previous visit, yet it was also very dark. Many boxes new and old were stacked next to the far wall. It looked as if he was moving.

"Good afternoon Mr. DePasqualle." I commented. DePasqualle turned his head and nodded continuing his rhythmic humming.

"Is Lord Burroughs in residence for our scheduled meeting today?" I asked DePasqualle. He casually pointed with his paintbrush to the chamber Lord Burroughs and myself had our previous meeting.

I walked hesitantly down the corridor towards Lord Burroughs chamber. A long Afghan rug covered the wooden floorboards keeping them from squeaking. The door separating Lord Burroughs chamber and the corridor was open slightly. Muffled noises of activity filtered from inside.

"Lord Burroughs?" I inquisitively asked pushing the chamber door open allowing myself room to enter.

Before me stood Sir Francis Lord Burroughs.

"Lord Burroughs!" I said startled at his condition, "You can walk. Why not a week had passed since I saw you confined to that wooden wheelchair. How has such a change in your condition occurred in such a limited time?"

"Confined? No, come in son. I am happy that you were able to join me on this auspicious day. It is a glorious day, is it not?" Lord Burroughs walked confidently towards me smiling, his mouth almost completely visible through the cotton mass still sticking to his face. He had shaven and his hair was trimmed. His hazel eyes had a sleepy antique look of an elderly statesman.

A neatly pressed buttoned down, pin-striped Oxford with the top button undone and the sleeves rolled a turn neatly tucked into a pair of charcoal, wool slacks held up by burgundy suspenders that matched the lustre of his polished shoes the heals of which knocked the white floor in a cocky rhythm as he walked. Disregarding the mass of cotton on his face, he looked much like a prominent businessman I had envisioned.

"Mr. DePasqualle is doing an exquisite job restoring my Lydia, don't you think? " Lord Burroughs asked.

"Yes. Of course. He has an artist's touch." I commented stunned at the much-improved appearance of this once degraded, humble old man.

"She will be very happy. Well, I've been occupied all this morning so I haven't seen the finishing touches, but I imagine with Marcus working on her it will be as beautiful as the day I painted her." Lord Burroughs walked to his writing desk in the corner of the wall and opened the leather diary and began jotting down an impromptu idea.

"Excuse me Lord Burroughs, but you haven't answered my question. This house, you, everything has so drastically changed..." I began to question but Lord Burroughs interrupted.

"A revelation. In our last conversation, we discussed love and fate. Correct?" Lord Burroughs questioned rhetorically. I nodded. "You mentioned how there are matches made in heaven. Correct?" He asked again his thoughts still concentrated on his ideas that he was writing in his diary.

"Yes." I gathered confused as to his inquisitive state and how it related to his seemingly miraculous recovery.

"Well, son," He turned to me with the wide-eyed excitement of a child, "there are matches made in heaven. The power that comes from that union is limitless and astounding. It encompasses all that we know and understand, all places and all times, all consciousness. It is forever." then he turned and continued with his thoughts inscribed in his diary.

"How does this coincide with this change?" I asked.

"Don't you see? It is so simple. I hadn't realized the answer until you, in your entire candor, mentioned it. I am eternally grateful." He smiled and shook my hand.

"I am flattered Lord Burroughs, but honestly I don't know exactly how I was of service." He looked at me astonished then chuckled shaking his head.

"You are quite the modest young man." He extended his diary opened to a peculiar drawing. "I have it partially built in this house, in the very basement on top of which we're standing."

I took hold of the diary and carefully inspected the ink drawing of some fantastic machine.

A pungent molded odor filled the darkness as we descended into this labyrinth beneath Lord Burroughs' home. The basement was extremely dark, void of any light except for what diffused through the crack beneath the stairway door, yet as I traveled further and further down the staircase the minuscule light did little favor. I paused a moment as I reached the landing that stretched out into the darkness.

"Hold there for a moment? It is dark, is it not?" I heard Lord Burroughs comment mixed with the knocking heals of his shoes. "Where's that switch?" Lord Burroughs said fumbling around in the darkness. Metal clanked together and a glass broke on the floor. Then there was light.

Reflections off the moist cobblestone floor. A long wooden workbench occupied the left wall. Tools littered the bench and saw dust lay indiscriminately on the floor, spread out by traveling feet. A large metallic tube with a faucet nozzle and several tubes attached to a metal wand were situated next to a large, grey mask with a very dark visor hanging off the tube. A rack of canned fruits sat dustily on a shelf to my right. Above me, the rafters were filled with cobwebs and coils of wire. The buzz of electricity ran through the wires to a generator that used steamed water heated to boiling by the abundant coal mound piled against the back wall next to the workbench. Lord Burroughs walked casually towards the object of his invention.

A half of a dozen lights pointed directly at this unfinished, magnificent machine. It was shiny like a knights' sword. An Egyptian pyramid came to mind as I admired Lord Burroughs invention. It was large enough for a man to stand erect with his arms held wide reminiscent of DaVinci's Vitruvian Man, the door obvious access for the intended use. Someone was going to be in this machine controlling the odd contraption by the two panels on either side of the interior. Blinking lights, knobs and levers covered the front of the panels fed by the deluge of wires leading into the bottom of each box cascading over the top of the machine tied to the iron beams constructing the machine. The wires then ran out and around the machine several times ending finally into a socket of the generator next to the workbench. To my left a lever struck out from a pillar absorbing the weight of many wooden, floor beams. It connected to the machine by multiple wires.

The moldy smell I once encountered was replaced by a strange combination of coal and electrical odor as I approached the machine. Lord Burroughs leaned against the machine proudly.

"What do you think?" Lord Burroughs asked

"I inspired you to build this?" I asked.

"Yes. It is the exact vision I had when we were speaking last week. Although extraordinarily crude, it resembles another invention I made, but this one is far superior. Strange I hadn't noticed that before." Lord Burroughs smiled and patted the object of his week's worth of hard work.

"What is it?" I asked.

"Well, that is a good question, is it not?" Lord Burroughs asked pulling up a chair cautiously sitting crossing his legs, "Perhaps I should qualify what I am about to show you with a bit of history." He ran his fingers through his hair, pained an expression and began his tale.

"Many years ago my wife, Lydia, was born near here. I believe it was known as the O'Connor mansion. We met while attending Cambridge our freshman year. She

64

studied English while I wasted my time in poetry and physics. She was more beautiful than anything I had ever known. I, being the hopeless romantic, delved into writing her endless, infantile verses dedicated to her beauty. For many months, I admired her from afar never attempting to meet her believing she would never have anything to do with me. I know that seems childish, doesn't it?" Lord Burroughs asked affirming his belief nodding his head.

"I don't think so." I answered not explaining my preoccupation with Jacqueline.

"You are understanding. That is one of the reasons why I continued to call upon you. It is not for what you know, but what you understand. Either way, chivalry had a brief revival amidst those lonely months. During this time, I encountered a man, which would come to be Mr. DePasqualle's father, William. He was knowledgeable in a science thought long to be extinct. That science was Theological Metaphysics: the belief in the eternal life and power of the human soul. What time do you have?" He asked walking to the machine. He glanced at his gold watch dangling on a gold chain from his pants pocket. He opened the door and walked in.

"It's 1:23." I answered looking at the gold wristwatch my parents gave to me for my acceptance to Cambridge University.

"When I say, you pull the lever to your immediate left, please?" his hands worked confidently on the panels. I could hear the wires above in the rafters buzz from behind me then pass into the machine. The lights dimmed and the odor of electricity and burning coal became overpowering. I squinted my eyes and sneezed several times. Inside, Lord Burroughs absorbed the bluish electrical light that arched from the panels across the outside of the machine.

"Yes, sir." I anxiously answered.

The coils of wire wrapped around the machine began to shake with the power and several containers of fruit fell from the shelves.

Above the increasing noise he yelled, "Pull the lever now, son."

The cobblestones beneath my feet shook and vibrated. As I reached for the lever I stumbled recovering my balance on the workbench only to find myself catching tools shaking off the countertop. With one final stretch, I fingered the edge of the lever slowly pulling it down. The sound increased ten-fold as did the light. I fell to the ground slipping on sawdust and cowered under the workbench waiting for the machine Lord Burroughs operated to explode or catch fire or some other incredible apocalyptic ending to this extraordinary device. My ovular spectacles struck against a leg of the workbench and landed in the pile of sawdust. I cupped my hands over my face and closed my eyes.

Everything became strangely quiet. As I opened my eyes Lord Burroughs was standing outside the machine patting it like an obedient dog delivering the morning paper to its master.

Carefully, I came from my protective shell beneath the workbench and crawled to meet Lord Burroughs standing above me his extended hand helping me to my feet. Behind him, the lever I had pulled was now pointing up. The disarray I encountered as Lord Burroughs powered the machine was completely gone.

"It is very powerful, this device is. Imagine how much more powerful it would be if the most powerful and pure source of energy known to man was surging through those wires." He crossed his arms confidently, "What time do you have now?"

I reached down and retrieved my glasses from the saw dust pile. Speckles of wood shavings covered the prescripted glass,   I brushed them off with a soft wipe of my cotton shirt. I replaced them to my head and look at my wristwatch. Strange. I quickly removed my spectacles and wiped them off again for the light covering of dust must have diluted my vision. What I was seeing surely was wrong. I replaced the spectacles to my head again and looked at my watch. 1:17 p.m. I shook my hand in hopes of adjusting the apparent mechanical problem occurring within the watch.

"What is wrong, son?" Lord Burroughs asked. He rubbed his chin creating a cottony shower falling from his face. Small balls of cotton landed in the sawdust. He didn't notice.

"I must've bumped my wrist watch on the leg of the workbench I was under. I seem to have lost a few minutes." I answered. Although I didn't remember hitting my hand or wrist certainly in the chaos during the last few moments it could have been broken.

"Really? Lost or gained?" Lord Burroughs asked inquisitively.

"Lost." I answered confused to his question. "My watch is off five minutes from the last time you asked me. It was 1:23 now it's 1:17. This watch never worked very well anyhow." I said although it wasn't true. I had dropped it many times since my parents bought it for me and it never lost its time, but with all that happened I guess I was surprised to still be alive.

"Your watch is fine, son. Come sit here." He pointed to a stool next to the machine.

I sat next to Lord Burroughs and he was quiet for a moment then he gently put his arm over my shoulders.

"I am sorry if I frightened you, son. I thought if I could show you how real it was then you would believe the rest of the story I am about to tell you." He discontinued and walked to the shelf of canned fruits, "I am glad to see all of the fruits have survived the chaos." He looked at me strangely, "Yes, these fruits will never fall from these shelves."

"Wait a moment." I interrupted. "I remember an entire container smashing on the ground."

"Oh, now you must've been mistaken. That is possible, is it not?" He questioned.

"No, I distinctly remember seeing and hearing a container crashing to the ground splattering the contents on the floor." I said as walked to the shelf examining the floor.

"And what time would that have been, when the container dropped to the floor?" Lord Burroughs grabbed my wrist and looked at my watch.

"Well, it would have been 1:23 or so..." I said trailing off.   "What exactly are you trying to say, Lord Burroughs?"

"I am saying you gained five minutes of your life." He said overjoyed.

"How is that possible? More than likely I merely struck my watch on the leg of the workbench and caused it to malfunction.. Briefly." I defensively said.

66

"Don't think of time as a linear, chronological order of events. Think of it as past, present and future all happening at one time just in different places. As you were in one place at 1:23 when the fruit crashed on the ground, you are now in another place at 1:17 where that event hasn't occurred yet. Time was minutely altered in the place you were while time was drastically changed where I was inside the machine." He described pulling the watch from his pocket. He opened the emblazoned, gold face and showed me the time he had. The watch read 7:17.

"Come. Let's see how Mr. DePasqualle is faring on Lydia. There is so much more to tell you." He led me upstairs where DePasqualle was finished removing the cotton that stuck into the painted Lydia.

My eyes took a moment to adjust to the light saturating the atrium where DePasqualle continued his restoration. He stepped back and admired his work. "She is as beautiful as the day you painted her, Francis." dePasqaulle exclaimed.

"And immortal." Lord Burroughs answered. He was tall and confident and his Lydia was reborn into a new light with the help of DePasqualle. She was eternally beautiful and I could without difficulty understand how Lord Burroughs became a disenfranchised man. Now she was here, again, and his world was quiet and right. He was one.

Outlining the inside of the atrium were dozens of boxes, some apparently full taped shut while others awaited their cargo. Lord Burroughs was leaving and very soon.

"Are you moving, Lord Burroughs?" I asked directed towards the array of boxes littering the floor.

"In a way, son." He casually put his hand upon my shoulder, smiled and said, "I'm putting my affairs in order. It wouldn't be kind to a very dear and personal friend as Mr. DePasqualle to leave many ends untied, would it? Things need to be arranged so as to not be difficult for Mr. DePasqualle to handle when I return."

"No, it wouldn't." I answered confusedly. Return? Return to where?

"You should be going, shouldn't you? We have an incredible day tomorrow. Can you be here at 11:00 a.m. in the morning?" He asked with smile I could not refuse.

"Of course Lord Burroughs. Will you finish the rest of this story then?" I asked.

"Tomorrow you will learn everything." He answered leading me out to the front door of is home. I shook his hand and promised I would return at 11:00 sharp tomorrow morning. Both DePasqualle and Lord Burroughs stood at the doorway waving good-bye as I peddled my bicycle away from 423 Manchester Drive toward Gray's Quadrangle.

The dormitory was unusually quiet this particular evening. Faces on the moon quietly smiled rising through the sleeping, autumnal oaks surrounding Gray's Quadrangle while a brisk, November wind sloughed the dying leaves into a corner of the dormitory like the huddling poor around a fire. There was a light on in my room.

I could see my door was ajar as I ventured down the solemn halls. Jeffrey Stephens occupied the room adjacent to mine and was a frequent guest and consummate prankster. He was about my age and height with sandy colored hair and a stocky build. Due to a wandering eye, he wore thick black glasses to correct his vision. His friends refereed to him as 'the Hawk', always on the lookout for a good laugh. I always called him Jeffrey, though. Perhaps it was just my imagination, but he smelled constantly of some condiment of which I could never discern.

It was legend that one of his great, great grandfathers was one of the perpetrators of Gray's death in 1771. This was something he was neither proud of nor embarrassed by. Simply family history. Obviously, some of the tomfoolery had been passed down through the generations. On occasion, I unfortunately played the surrogate Gray for his pranks. I readied myself this day.

Placing my hands on the oak trim outlining my door, I jumped through sliding quickly under any traps or surprise attacks awaiting my arrival stopping just shy of my mattress with my head looking under my bed. Rolling over to my back, I cowered for a brief moment glancing anxiously around the room. Overhead, the Hawk smiled hanging his mop of sandy hair over the edge of the bed.

"A little late for spring cleaning, don't you think?" he asked disappearing back onto the bed. I could hear him chuckling.

"I can't take any chances." I said standing, brushing myself off. "Besides, it took me a week to clean-up all the water you threw on me last time and I went ahead and cleaned the entire floor so the joke's on you."

"Jumping through the door like a scared cat really taught me a lesson." he rolled his good eye sarcastically.

"What are you doing in my room, Jeffrey?" I asked walking to my desk pulling out a chair to sit.

"I was bored so I thought I'd see what you were up to. Now I see it must be gymnastics." he said smugly situating himself up against the headboard while crossing his feet. He tossed a football into the air like a quarterback acting as if he were a star football player. Perhaps Jeffrey might have made a first-rate football player had he been a slight larger and had better eyes. For now he settled for friendly games between rival dormitories and throwing around the football with me. I was his only true friend.

"Well, I've..." I hesitated thinking of my answer. Not only was Jeffrey known as a consummate prankster but an atrocious busybody. "...been busy with school."

"Uh-huh. Still writing love letters to... what was her name? Gertrude? Beatrice? What?" he asked already knowing the answer for it was he who made my infatuation with Jacqueline the source of much inconsideration.

"You know well enough that it was Jacqueline and no, I wasn't writing her love letters. As I said I have been busy with school. Some of us do attend school regularly, you know." I remarked pointedly at his penchant for hooky.

"I am learning by osmosis." he commented looking slightly guilty of the charge. In actuality, he needn't attend school for he was rather intelligent and his family was quite wealthy with many connections. Jeffrey had ambitions, but they weren't directed towards anything. He smirked and asked, "Hey, how's theology coming?"

"B-" I reluctantly answered. Now Jeffrey was well aware that my grades in Theology were inferior to his. For some unexplained, preternatural reason he was able to pull A's from professor Favret like candy from a child without attending a lecture and he loved to affirm his superiority.

"With grades like that they'll have to start calling you St. Augustine." he added tossing the football for punctuation.

"At least I am one up on you in Latin, you apple polisher." I rebounded. Jeffrey was a half a grade lower than I. "With grades like you get they'll have to start calling you Thomas Gray." The 'Thomas Gray' comment was always the clincher. Having said that, I knew he wouldn't have much to say in return.

He defeatedly smiled and sat quiet for a moment. He broke his silence with, "You want to throw around the football for a while?"

"I can't, I have to study." I didn't actually need to study, but wanted some time to myself.

"Yea, me too." he slipped from the bed with this football and turned toward the door. He paused for a second and turned, "You know my family didn't kill Gray. He killed himself."

"What do you mean? He died of pneumonia from the romp in the water your grandfather pushed under his window." I argued.

"No, that was only the effect. Everyone, faculty included, knew there was something wrong with him. All those hours spent writing Latin, secluded in that cramped room next door." he paused cleaning his glasses pointing to Gray's museum in the next room. It was amazing how much his glasses masked his wandering eye. "No one falls for the same trick seven times, not even a kook like Gray." he returned his glasses to his face. "You know when he died they went to package his belongings and put his writings in order and you know what they found?" he asked

"No." I answered.

"His affairs in order." he said with a hint of implication.

"So, he was a tidy man" I said dismissing such conspiracy.

"Not tidy, suicidal. His will, where he wanted to be buried, notes to friends pending his death, everything detailed, written on paper stuffed in an envelope address 'To Whom It May Concern'. He was waiting to die, waiting for the next false fire drill so he could plunge to his death. Little did he know it would take him weeks to die, drowning in his own lungs." He paused as if feeling slightly responsible.

"I've heard rumors surrounding his death. Suicide seemed to be swept under the carpet, but every now and again I'd hear something, but out of respect most people let it drop." I said easing the situation.

"Now you know." he looked around the room avoiding eye contact for this was his patented look ever since I met him out side the dormitory my freshman year. The minute he became angry, he'd avoid eye contact and make-up some absurd excuse to leave the room as quickly as possible. As a matter of fact, he did this very maneuver the first day I met him. Although, this was after I mistakenly referred to him as 4-eyes. Regrettably, it somewhat tainted our friendship bent more upon a cordial suspicion than trust.

"And that's exactly what happened?" I questioned Jeffrey as if it was a tall tale.

"Yes. Why would I make-up such a thing about a dead man?" he asked in an aggravated tone.

"You wouldn't, Jeffrey. I was just fooling around." I walked towards him to ease the moment.

69

"Well, I have to..." Jeffrey paused momentarily finding a suitable excuse, "...shine my shoes before class begins." and with that, he left my room. I closed the door behind him.

Lord Burroughs stood before me dressed in a long, white bedgown drenched in blood with his fists clenched. Screaming, wailing, his blood stained my room like raining spiderwebs. From the pitch black hallway miles of wire slithered in wrapping around his body and neck until his throat could no longer sustain his screams. Several wires burrowed through his crossed ankles and into his wrists lifting his body off the wooden floor. A cabled halo crushed his skull from the constricting pressure of the wire serpents. Droplets of blood ran from his forehead like rain. Christ incarnate, the serpentine wires raised him farther into the heavens until he disappeared in a overpowering blue light so beautiful my eyes could not blink for fear of losing the vision of his soul ascending to heaven where his Lydia waits to.... and the dream was over.

My chest heaved under my bedshirt sticky with sweat. I raised from my bed and walked to the windows swinging one open allowing a brisk breath of air to whisk in from outdoors. The smell of chill and leaves burns my memory. I was stunned by the dream.

As I looked at the ground below, the aberrant dream slowly faded from my mind. While watching the leaves scurry across the ground like spiders waiting for spring, I could imagine poor Gray splashing awkwardly in the reservoir of water while onlookers, like Jeffrey's grandfather, sinfully laughed, showing their smiling, hurtful barbs. How lonely he must have been to commit suicide while so young. I wondered if anyone had seen the signs or noticed something that might have prevented his unwarranted death. Boxes arduously packed to help his survivors, his will, papers for his burial rights, all his affairs in order.

The November chill calmed my uncertain nerves as I closed the window and slowly walked back to my bed. Suddenly, I stopped at the edge of my footboard as a strange feeling overcame me, call it an understanding of something Lord Burroughs had mentioned earlier:

'I'm putting my affairs in order. It wouldn't be kind to a very dear and personal friend as Mr. DePasqualle to leave so many ends untied, would it? Things need to be arranged as to not be difficult for Mr. DePasqualle to handle when I return.'

It sounded so strange when he first uttered those words, but now it all made sense. Just as Gray's loneliness and isolation ended his life, living without Lydia was more than Lord Burroughs could endure. The machine, that incredible invention which bends time, was to him as Gray's icy cold waters beneath his dormitory window; an end to his growing, solitary pain.

Constructed in his cellar, the metallic machine cowered in the corner solemnly out of sight waiting to withdraw the draining spirit from Lord Burroughs body. His soul

70

freed to follow the brilliantine light of heavens gate where his dear Lydia awaited her true love. Made of the finest materials and with the greatest of care, the machine was nothing more than an elaborate noose designed to ease the idea of killing himself.   And there it was. I understood now and as of tomorrow at 1:00, I would witness the suicide of Sir Francis Lord Burroughs.

That night I would watch the cold, dark night slowly crawl into shadows fearing the fiery arrival of the morning sun.

As I readied myself for the meeting with Lord Burroughs, an overwhelming feeling of despair overcame me like canvas sackcloth.

I left the dormitory early as it took me a full hour to walk to his home. Riding my bicycle allowed me to arrive at Lord Burroughs' home too quickly for I wanted to fend off the oncoming meeting as long as possible.

As I turned onto Manchester Lane, the sun hid behind a cloud moving toward the rapidly decaying home. I witnessed a face from behind a curtain spying me from inside a house lining the cobblestone lane. Its eyes darkened with suspicion and conjecture. I hung my head in sadness and drove my hands deep inside the thick pockets of my blue, autumn jacket warming them from the enveloping chill of the sunless residence. Slate roof tiles increasing accumulated on the front lawn from the forward slant of the roof. The sound of the constant shifting of tiles sounded like a glacier tearing away topsoil. Beneath, the wrens had completely devoured the rose bushes as only thorny sticks drove from the infertile soil ever defensive against the onslaught of dandelions and ivy. Before I knocked on the front door, the rotting floorboards creaked and the heavy, wooden door simultaneously opened with Lord Burroughs standing fully inside the doorway. He was smiling and healthy, his face completely cleared of the guilt induced cotton mask.

"Come in son, you're early." he gently placed his hand upon my shoulder. It had a quiet strength in its fingers as it eased my growing feeling of ill. He led me into his home, its contents packed away in boxes lining the interior. The air was fresh with cleaning pine and oil paint. I casually glanced at the mural of the newly restored Lydia and she was angelic. Long flowing, golden hair draped her shoulders while her smile humored some timeless joke. Below her windswept paisley summer dress, flower pixies slept entranced by her beauty. She, even as a rendering, was eternally beautiful and I could imagine even the gifted, artistic touch of Mr. DePasqualle was not able to completely capture her peaceful elegance.

"Today is a most important day in both our lives, son." Lord Burroughs added, his voice passionate. "Come, let's retire to my chamber. We have many things to discuss." eagerly, he showed me into his private sanctuary.

Inside, his chamber was almost completely barren. One solitary calendar stuck to the white wall with 'Lydia at 1:00' printed in red marker. His desk, loveseat and diary were nowhere to be seen. Only two rickety, wooden chairs stood in the chamber ensconced in white facing each other. Here, we discussed the preparation for his return.

71

"At exactly 1:00, I will be inside operating the machine. Then when I tell you to pull the lever, you do so. No later or earlier or there might be dire consequences. Do you understand?" he was very serious in his questioning.

"Yes, I understand, Lord Burroughs." I answered. I was so preoccupied with my own questions that I could barely concentrate on his instructions.

"You allowed me to discover the power for my return. It was all completely in front of my eyes and I still could not see it. I knew you would be a special person when we first met." He paused for a moment with seriousness in his eyes. "I will not see you after you pull the lever and I will miss you dearly, for it is you who offered me the insight into my dilemma. Without your understanding, I could never have returned to my Lydia. I thank you for this and I regret I can never repay you or can I?"

"Yes, you can, Lord Burroughs, by answering several questions I have that I cannot find an answer to." I said almost exasperated.

"Absolutely, son..." suddenly, he looked at his watch and noticed the impending time ticking away. "but you'll have to ask your questions while we venture to the cellar, do you mind?"

"No, I don't mind, sir."

"You'll have to hurry, it is almost time, son." he said looking at his watch again.

Lord Burroughs' steps were hurried and sure as I followed close behind. We passed dear Lydia on our way to the cellar. She was completely restored and beautiful. Her eyes followed our gathered steps. I readied myself for the coming conversation from which I would receive the answers to the questions that splintered my mind. Then I realized that of all the questions I once had, I could only recall one.

"Lord Burroughs?" I asked as we traveled down the dimly lit cellar stairs. He glanced back at me inviting the questions. "Where do you intend to return to?" I continued.

We both stopped at the end of the stairwell and he answered, "The future." and he continued walking towards the magnificent machine.

"The future?" I confusedly asked.

"Yes, the machine I have built is a time machine. It is beautiful, isn't it? " he smiled as he turned the remaining lights on directed towards the machine.

"Yes, it is very beautiful, but a time machine, sir. I don't understand." I was very confused as I walked towards the machine with Lord Burroughs easing himself into the pod.

"I created a time machine to help cure the disease that took my beloved Lydia from me. It is incurable and extremely contagious in my time, so I constructed a machine out of theory and metal to transport me to the past in effort to beat the disease before it becomes an epidemic. I had time on my side, but God had failed me in my attempt to change the tides of fate and he punished me." his face was very grim and disconcerted. He pulled cords of rope and wire into the machine tightly.

"He punished you for what, sir?" I asked helping him arrange the wires.

"When Lydia had found out she was infected, we knew there wasn't much time. I devoted the entire time she had left on this Earth to finding a cure, but I was too late. I came to the conclusion that the only cure is to beat the disease before it tore across the world in a pestilent wave. Marcus DePasqualle had died decades earlier, yet his son was very knowledgeable in physics, chemistry and theological metaphysics. With his help I was able to construct a machine similar to this one. When I traveled back through time, I used Lydia's soul to power the machine. She had such a will to live and she was so powerful that when I arrived on a Tuesday at 1:00 in the past a tear in the space-time continuum occurred and...." he paused. From inside, he started the machine. The noise continued to build.

"So what happened? Please continue?" I pleaded. Whirring and buzzing saturated the air as a swift smell of ozone gathered above my head.

"Do you know about the O'Connor fire where the mother and her unborn child were caught in the blaze and died shortly thereafter?" he said over the noise as he stopped his preparations and leaned on the metal beams.

I nodded yes.

"That unborn child was my Lydia." his eyes began well and he looked away. "Not only had I wasted the time I had left with Lydia, I destroyed her complete existence. I tried to continue on with my life, but all I could manage to do was give this time a few of the luxuries that my time developed and ......" his voice was slowly drowning out under the gaining rumble of the time machine. Then he glanced at his watch and looked at my with widened eyes and yelled, "Two minutes!"

I remembered his instructions and I walked quickly toward the lever. As I placed my hands on the lever readying myself, something occurred to me.

"Lord Burroughs," I yelled. He turned toward me in an effort to better hear me. "If Lydia was the power for the time machine that brought you here, what will power your voyage home?" I asked barely audible over the incredible power of the machine.

"I Am Not Returning Home, Son. I'm Returning to Lydia." he answered very loudly.

"But She Doesn't Exist." I countered.

He looked at his watch and yelled, "THIRTY SECONDS!"

"I SAID SHE DOESN'T EXIST, Lord Burroughs!" I said again and it was in his eyes when he turned to me.

"SHE EXISTS IN HEAVEN, SON." and he looked into my eyes for what seemed an eternity. This machine was nothing more than an elaborate noose. All of the calendars I had seen when we first met had 'Tuesday at 1:00' written on them. He must have tried to end his pain every Tuesday and like Thomas Gray, but he needed an elaborate escape from his lonely existence. He knew all along he wasn't going to return, but it was my own lost love Jacqueline that fueled his mind to create this machine to end his life. The pain he had endured.

"I UNDERSTAND!" I yelled and he knew I truly did.

"TEN SECONDS!" he said beginning the countdown to one.

The increasing sound was now completely drowning out all other sounds. Cracks and snaps of electricity popped over my head leading to the machine as Lord Burroughs frantically controlled the interior knobs and buttons. As he pushed the last sequence of buttons a wire writhed loose from the metal of the mighty time machine.

Lord Burroughs noticed immediately as if it were a part of his self. His eyes wide with helplessness.

He pointed quickly to the wire and said, "RE-ATTACH THE WIRE TO THE METAL OR THERE WILL BE A FEEDBACK LOOP OUTSIDE OF THE MACHINE WHICH WILL CAUSE YOU TO BE...." I squinted to hear the last of his words but to no avail. I left my post at the lever immediately scampering to find the light gauge wire which broke loose, but it was gone somewhere in the light layer of saw dust on the floor. I looked up to see Lord Burroughs floating inside the pod engulfed in a blue light so brilliant it rivaled that of the bluest oceans and the widest sky combined. I was in awe.

"FIVE SECONDS!" he screamed over the deafening whir.

I ran over to the tool bench against the wall running my hands across the surface landing upon a pair of pliers covered in dust that closed tightly in the pressure of my hand.

"IT'S TIME. PULL THE LEVER! PULL THE LEVER--NOW!" His hands stretched out toward the lever, his face beautiful.

I glanced over at the lever and with one bounding leap grasped the lever with both hands pulling it down completing the circuit. The increased electricity surged like a deluge from a broken dam.

My skin burned from the brilliant light emanating from inside the time machine where Lord Burroughs became no longer visible. Out side the pod the wire flapped against the energy. I pushed with all my strength against the tremendous energy pulsing in and around the pod. Extending my hands with the pliers, I managed to grasp the wire in the crotch of the teeth connecting it to the metal bar and a blast of energy threw me across the floor where I lay unconscious inches from the fruit preserves.

I am not positive how long I lay unconscious on the cobblestone floor, but when I awoke my surroundings were altered. No longer were there fruit preserves littering these shelves above me. The entire basement was barren. Smoke and residual smells were gone, no saw dust or wires and the time machine was also gone. Lord Burroughs was no longer here, either. He had made his incredible journey to his destiny with Lydia, his timeless love awaiting him in heaven or some probable future I will never encounter. My thoughts were with him as I traveled up the cellar stairs removing myself from this empty grave.

The smell traveling from the atrium was fresh and green. I quickened my steps as I landed in the atrium of bare walls. The Lydia I had come to know had vanished, her rendering erased from the magenta walls as were the cotton faeries asleep under her enchantment. The packed boxes of Lord Burroughs 'affairs' were gone. Everything that was Sir Francis Lord Burroughs had disappeared along with the lonely recluse.

I had to relieve myself of this delirium for I found the front door quickly only to be momentarily blinded by the summer sky.

Azure grass stretched boundlessly beside Manchester Lane while vibrant, pastel tulips swayed carelessly in the August breeze so sweet I could recall the very first time I breathed it in. It was during my freshmen year, just before I first lain eyes upon Jacqueline. I smiled as I recalled her face again. If only I had more time, I thought. I left the residence of the late Lord Burroughs and walked down the path toward Manchester Lane with my hands deep inside my blue, autumn jacket. My hands warm inside those pockets as a bead of sweat dripped from my brow. I wiped it from my eyes with my hand and I stared at it at length.

I turned to spy the decaying, diseased home I had frequented to find a very well cared for house. Its crisp lines reminiscent of a new home as red roses in full bloom hovered above the thriving grass below a porch so strong Samson could not budge its granite pillars. The slate roof complete and safe under the blazing sun as robins and jays chirped happily, their bills full of grubs and worms. Everything I had come to know in the past weeks was different, new. I turned and ran.

I could see Gray's dormitory in the distance. Students were walking and talking everywhere around the dormitory I stayed. I was amazed at all the activity and my preoccupation caused me to bump into a fellow about my size.

"I am so sorry, my friend. Can I help you up?" I asked extending my hand.

His sandy hair hung over his bespectacled face as I helped him to his feet. He looked at me with an indifferent face, one I had seen so very often.

"Jeffrey," I said, "Are you alright?"

He looked at me confused.

"Do I know you?" Jeffrey asked, his eye wandering off in some mysterious direction.

"Of course you do you bespectacled, four..." and I paused. This wasn't Jeffrey, at least not the Jeffrey I had come to know. He didn't have that suspicious look on his face, that glimmer of mischievous in his lips. This was the Jeffrey I had first met.

This wasn't right. Everything around me was different, so vibrant, so new, but it wasn't new it was the past, the very first day of my freshmen year. Those very first words between Jeffrey and I tainted our friendship for years. He was always self-conscious about his raven-rimmed glasses.

The incredible energy that sent Lord Burroughs back to his Lydia somehow sent me back in time. I was touching the machine when it finally surged. Somehow I conducted a minute amount of flux from the machine which sent me back through the ether. I looked at my watch recalling the first incident when Lord Burroughs showed me the awesome power of the time machine. It had stopped a few seconds past 1:00.

I was so entirely overwhelmed by what had transpired that I had completely forgot to shake Jeffrey's hand.

"Hello" I said, my grip firm.

"Jeffrey Stephens." he reciprocated.

"I am so dreadfully sorry about this, honestly, I wasn't looking around and...." I started to apologize, but he jumped in.

"No, that's alright, I was cleaning my glasses when I dropped them and I wasn't looking where I had bent over. I have this wandering eye and... " Jeffrey's hand was welcoming and firm as he rambled on concerning his disabilities.

"That's alright." I confirmed and he just smiled.

"Where are you staying this year?" I asked and as Jeffrey pointed to Gray's dormitory, my eyes followed his direction and unexpectedly landed on the face I had so completely remembered.

Before me stood Jacqueline Elisabeth Haley.

"Excuse me for a moment, Jeffrey, would you?" I didn't wait for his reply as I walked past him to met Jacqueline.

I knew her more as I got closer. Everything about her was completely memorized.

Because of a family affliction called, Uncertainty, I was deprived of ever knowing her, yet the idle mind I fought so hard to occupy now allows me a second chance at an idea. Call it intuition, call it karma, call it foolish, but this time I would know her and she would know me.

She spied me as I approached her. A smile lit her face.

"Hello." I said my heart beating heavily in my chest. Certainly my face was flush.

She looked at me strangely for a moment and said, "Have we met?" her voice thick with southern garnish.

"No." I answered staring into her eyes. Her enveloping gaze never faltered.

"Are you sure?" she asked, "I could swear we've met before. Another place or time possibly?"

"That's entirely possible." I answered. I knew it was brash and uncertain, but I asked anyway, "I know this is rather sudden, but would you accompany me to the freshmen social this evening?"

She tucked a tuft of hair behind her ear and fell shy for a moment and answered, "I would be delighted!"

The cold, November evenings no longer chilled me that way they did in the past. I have her hand in mine and her smile in my heart as we trudge through the masses of dried, summer leaves on our way to the library. I make her laugh and she makes me whole and certain, more than I could ever have done on my own. Perhaps Lord Burroughs had seen a little of himself in me in that short time we knew each other and the gift he gave me I can never repay. Some day, I realize we shall meet again in a better time and place, but my time now and forever will always be with Jacqueline.

www.ingramcontent.com/pod-product-compliance
Lightning Source LLC
Chambersburg PA
CBHW021131130626
46554CB00002B/956